The Mouth

By Henry Anderson

Dedication
To my mother and father

The Mouth

Henry Anderson

ALL RIGHTS RESERVED

Publisher's Note:

This is a work of fiction. All names, characters, places, and events are the work of the author's imagination.

Any resemblance to real persons, places, or events is coincidental.

Solstice Publishing - www.solsticepublishing.com

Part I: The War Machines

Chapter One
Badger

The sound of war machines drifted out of the shattered suburbs.

The boy looked upriver towards the old brick bridge whose shallow arches were faintly sketched in the morning mist.

He ripped the patchwork blanket from around his shoulders and tossed it into the swift, clay-brown water. The cloth pulsated for a heartbeat before the tide swept it away. He hesitated for a second and threw his fishing rod after it.

Then he turned to the sloping flood bank behind him. Wild flowers had colonized the old concrete wall. He caught hold of some long grass and swung himself up into the valley.

The lumbering war machines shook the earth so hard his teeth rattled.

A faint mist hung over the valley.

A line of olive-green tanks advanced over the old bridge.

He looked across a frost-whitened wasteland. On the other side there was a steep hill made of pulverised masonry and human bones.

Someone shouted something and fired a rifle at him. He ran between stunted trees and scrub bushes to the foot of the hill.

Behind him, diesel exhaust from the tanks was darkening the morning mist.

Soldiers ran over the bridge. Their ragged uniforms were stained with mud and ash. Their faded light-blue berets identified them as the Royal Curfew Regiment.

He took a winding track up the ruined slope. His boot snagged on the wheel of a bicycle and he fell into the mud.

He heard a voice in the valley give the order to fire. A bullet hit the path a few inches above his head. He rolled sideways and tumbled down over steel girders and rotten timber until he hit the bottom of an ancient bomb crater.

He lay still for a few seconds and listened to the rifles in the valley. Then he crawled up to the wall of the depression and peered between the branches of a blackthorn bush. The tanks had formed a line on the riverbank. Soldiers lay between them, rifles pointed at the hill. Puffs of smoke floated above their heads.

A group of cavalry officers trotted their horses over the wasteland. The men wore white pith helmets.

A fat soldier waved foxhounds from a Bedford lorry.

A square hatch stuck out of the rubble wall. A smell of damp cellar drifted out.

A voice said, "Jack?"

A man clambered out of the hole. He had a long white face and a mass of dark grey hair that fell over the fur collar of a long black coat.

Jack said, "Sorry, Badger, I didn't know you lived here."

Badger crawled over and stared through a pair of ROSS PRISM binoculars. Down in the valley several men in reflective heat suits were strapping doughnut-shaped fuel packs on their back. Their silver uniforms glowed yellow in the early sun.

Badger said, "Ferrets."

A hatch opened in a Centurion tank. A man stood up and held an electronic loud hailer to his mouth.

He said, "Good morning. I am Brigadier-General Augustine Champion, the Prince of Wales. This area is in permanent curfew. I am here on behalf of my father to rescue you from maladaptive behaviour patterns."

Badger spat onto the crater floor. Jack took the binoculars. The General's pale grey eyes were magnified by a pair of round spectacles. The man waited a few seconds, lowered the loudhailer and then disappeared into his tank, closing the hatch behind him.

The armoured vehicle's seventeen-pound turret gun fired a shell.

It hit a porcelain bathtub a few feet from the crater. The shock wave knocked them both onto the ground. Shrapnel and masonry roared around them.

Jack felt Badger's boots on his back as the older man scrambled out of the hollow.

Rifles fired.

Jack tore up the crater wall towards the bomb-damaged houses further up the hill, the words *I must not trip, I must not stumble* running constantly through his mind like a prayer.

Butterfly bushes flourished in the abandoned back gardens of ruined terraced houses. The walls that still stood were burnt black by incendiary bombs.

A bullet nicked Jack's sleeve. He saw Badger's long legs jumping between heaps of masonry.

The forest was a dark line ahead of them.

An explosion blew a cream-coloured trolleybus into the side of a house.

Badger disappeared into the woods.

A bullet smacked into a window frame by Jack's feet. He climbed up a heap of rubble and jumped into the treeline.

Birch saplings broke his fall.

Soon he was sprinting amongst the old, broad-leaved trees of the Weald.

The noise behind him died away.

His boots crunched on frozen leaf mould.

Two notes from a horn sounded in the air. Badger stepped out from behind the bulbous trunk of an old beech tree.

"What was that?" said Jack.

"Death."

Sweat steamed from Badger's hair.

He said, "They won't want to do us straight off. Those fellers like to take their time."

"What can we do?"

"When I was a kid, my old man used to lay something on the ground to put them off the scent, like wild garlic. Or a blood trail. The dogs like blood, you see."

Jack pulled a string necklace out of his jumper. A key hung from it.

"I know a place near here where we can hide," he said.

The older man shook his head.

"No time, they'll be here in a minute."

Badger reached into his coat and pulled out a long bayonet. It had a wooden handle. The blade looked old but the edges shone. For a moment Jack thought of the days that he had hunted and laughed with this man.

Badger said, "Sorry," and thrust the blade forward. Jack dodged sideways and grabbed the tall man's wrist. He used the grip as a crazy leverage to hoist himself into the air. His feet hovered for a moment. Then he stamped on Badger's knee.

Dogs raced through the woods. A cavalry officer made a hollering sound. One of his colleagues blew a horn.

Jack took cover behind an ancient oak tree, grabbed the lowest branch and swung himself up.

The barking of the pack was joyous and high-pitched.

Badger staggered to his feet and waved his knife at them, saying, "Get away, now. Go on."

The hum of a twelve-cylinder diesel engine filled the forest and the long gun of a war machine nosed through the trees.

The foxhounds circled their prey. One jumped up and bit at Badger's throat. He grabbed the animal by its ears and stabbed his blade into its neck. Blood sprayed over the ring of dogs.

Three men galloped up. One kicked Badger's face with the heel of his boot. The sweating man grunted and dropped into the seething pack of animals.

The Centurion halted and Prince Augustine shouted, "Hey lads, are you having some sport?"

A ruddy-cheeked horseman rode over to the tank and said, "Yes thank you, your Highness."

The hounds swarmed over Badger while he tried to fend them off with flicks of his arms and legs.

The Prince watched the tall man struggle and said, "Wish I was on horseback and not cooped up in this bloody tin can."

The young officer laughed loudly and said, "We all wish you were too, sir. We could use your expertise."

"Good man."

Prince Augustine got back into his tank and the vehicle moved off.

The red-faced officer shouted something at the pack. The animals retreated a few paces.

Badger sat up. His right cheek had been torn open and he was missing the top half of one ear. His blade was gone.

The soldier said, "Get up, or I'll kill you with my bare hands."

Badger got to his feet and said, "I'd like to see you try."

The young officer pulled out a silver pocket watch.

"We'll give you a sporting chance, something you didn't give the dog. You have two minutes," he said.

Jack dropped onto the ground and ran, keeping the big oak between himself and the soldiers.

He came to a heaped triangle of stacked tree trunks abandoned for decades in front of an impenetrable hedgerow.

The tank stopped moving. The turret swiveled towards Jack and the front machine gun fired.

Jack ran up the pile of timber. The logs were slippery with frost. Bullets tore into the wood. He launched himself over the hedge and fell onto a moss-covered pavement on the other side.

His brother had called this place the Haunted Village. The untended cherry and plane trees lining the streets had matured into a forest, burying the former suburb in permanent gloom.

Rain drummed on the branches that arched over the streets.

The rusted hulk of a Morris Oxford motorcar stood outside one of the houses. A fallen lamppost had cut the roof in half, showering the front garden with red tiles.

He climbed through the drawing room window over a sofa that had rotted down to rags and rusty springs. A picture of a steam train hung above the fireplace. Years ago, he sat on the floor and read books by Arthur Ransome and T.H. White.

A stalactite of ice hung above a cluster of ferns growing between the floorboards.

The Centurion smashed through the overgrown hedgerow.

Prince Augustine's amplified voice said, "This is the Royal Curfew Regiment. Surrender immediately or you will be shot. It is your responsibility."

Jack flattened himself and crawled over the rotten floor. The tank opened fire. He climbed out of the back window and ran into the forest.

There was a tall cone-shaped roof among the trees. His brother had claimed the chimney for drying hops was a fake, added by the old Ministry of Defence.

The house stood between a walled kitchen garden and an apple orchard. The window frames were lilac coloured and every pane of glass was unbroken. A neat frost-covered lawn glistened in the sun.

There was a stone patio. A man with a double chin and a shaved head stared out of some French windows. He wore a white vest.

Jack ran across the lawn and opened the glass door.

A Noel Coward record was playing on a gramophone.

A woman cried out. She had curlers in her grey hair.

A coal fire burnt in the grate.

The man dived behind a leather sofa.

A young red-haired woman grabbed a poker from beside the coals and waved it around.

The man stood up and pointed a shotgun at Jack.

"You appear to have lost your way."

"I just want to use the cellar."

"This is a wonderful old house. We have to defend it from riff-raff."

The older woman said, "We live very simply here. But we do eat very well."

Jack said, "There's a snatch squad outside."

The man in the vest said "Nonsense. Out into the garden. Move."

They walked outside. The woods were silent.

"Not a bloody peep. Nice try."

"All I want is the cellar."

"How'd you know about that?"

"My parents were in the Resistance. My father was killed here."

"He was an idiot then. Move or I'll shoot you."

They stopped outside the high walls of the kitchen garden. The man in the vest kicked a dilapidated wooden door open. Brick pathways ran between beds of frozen earth. An old greenhouse had condensation on its windows.

The man said, "Kneel."

His heavy breathing was the only noise in the garden.

"It was you who squealed, wasn't it? There were good people down there," Jack said.

"I had no choice."

An amplified voice in the garden said, "This area is under permanent curfew."

Jack grabbed the gun barrel. The weapon fired and made a hole in the frozen earth.

The man ran to the house. Jack followed him into a kitchen where the woman in curlers hugged her daughter. The man took cartridge shells from a box under the sink.

He pointed at Jack and said, "Stay there!"

There was a tinkling sound as the French windows were kicked in.

Jack ran down a long hallway lined with paintings and vases. His mother had told him there would be a cupboard door beneath the stairs. He opened it. There was a row of coats hanging from a rail. He swept them aside.

Gold lettering painted on a blue door said, H.M. GOVERNMENT. NO ENTRY.

There were footsteps in the hallway. He snapped the string around his neck and put the key in the lock.

A voice in the corridor said, "Royal Curfew Regiment. Drop the gun, now!"

The man with the shaved head said, "We have an agreement with Mede College, London!"

Jack pushed the metal door open and went into the darkness behind it.

He heard the older woman say, "The terrorist is in the cupboard. We have nothing to do with him."

A pistol went off. The younger woman screamed. The gun fired two more shots.

There was no light for Jack to navigate by. He ran his fingers over blistered paintwork. The toe of his boot clanged on the metal tread of a staircase.

He held onto the bannisters and took the steps three at a time until the stairs ended and he fell into a pool of freezing water.

It smelled foul.

Jack pictured the map his mother made him memorize. This area was called the FUEL FARM.

He heard boots on the stairs.

A voice shouted, "Royal Curfew Regiment. We know you are down here. Give yourself up."

Jack opened a door into what he hoped was OFFICES AND DEPARTMENTS.

He held up his grandfather's brass lighter. Typewriters and telephones lay in dark, ankle-deep water. There was a green and black tidemark on the whitewashed walls. A calendar on a desk said 7 JULY 1948.

He splashed into the RAF OPS CENTRE. It had a high ceiling. There was an elevated balcony overlooking two circular map tables. The floor was dry here.

Shouts and barking echoed along the corridor. A sign said: THE GPO TELEPHONE EXCHANGE. The room was long and narrow. The tiled walls had been smashed up by gunfire. Telephone cords hung from abandoned switchboards.

He opened a door with a sign saying WOMEN'S DORMITORY. The room had a few upturned beds. There was a long row of metal cupboards. He walked up to one of them and opened it. There was a false section of plaster wall which he pushed to one side. He squeezed through the rectangular space that had opened up and then leant back to lock the door from the inside.

Jack held his lighter up. The little room was covered in dust. There was a single armchair. A chess set had been set up on the floor. The black and white pieces were in their opening positions.

Cold air came out of a ventilation grill on the back wall.

He sat down.

A dog barked in the women's dormitory. Someone tried to open a few metal cupboards and then gave up.

He closed his eyes.

Chapter Two
The Bridge

Jack woke hanging upside down. He was still in the chair but it had been flipped over and lay wedged against a wall. A second later, he slumped onto the floor. There was too much dust and smoke to catch a proper breath. He crawled out.

There were piles of brick and plaster on the floor. The wall with the metal cupboards was gone.

His ears were ringing.

He pulled the grill out of the back wall and climbed out into a ventilation shaft. A giant fan lay over a pile of rotted-out bricks and cement. The dark chimney went up hundreds of feet.

There was a metal ladder on the wall. It swayed with each step.

He climbed for a couple of minutes up to a vent shed. The floor had collapsed and fallen down the shaft, leaving only a ragged concrete ledge.

The metal walls of the structure bulged under the weight of outside vegetation.

A blast of scorching air blew up the tunnel. It smelled of petroleum and enveloped him in burning ashes.

The thin ledge was covered in frozen moss. Jack splayed his feet and shuffled to a door. The handle came off in his hand.

He put his shoulder against the wall and shoved. There was a rending noise. The hut fell onto its side, leaving him standing in the night air.

Someone pointed a torch at him. A gun fired. The bullet ricocheted down the shaft.

A voice said, "Stay where you are, Curfew Rat!"

A shadowy form ran towards him.

Jack jumped over the hole and slid over the collapsed shed.

The figure slipped on the mossy ledge of the vent shaft and dropped down the tunnel. There was a wet thud.

The house with the cone-shaped roof was burning. On the lawn, a mobile fire unit of shiny-suited ferrets drank mugs of tea.

Jack weaved between the trees of the dark forest until he smelt tobacco smoke and lay flat on the earth. The orange tip of a cigarette brightened and then disappeared behind a cupped hand.

A bird fluttered in the treetops. In front of him, an animal trail led to the old tarmac road. The scent of human waste wafted from a latrine.

He heard a twig snap behind him and ran forward. Ahead of him, a silhouetted war machine was dark against moonlit clouds.

A canvas squad tent had been erected in front of the tank. Someone inside was snoring.

The soldiers had set up three twelve-feet-high black poles beside the road. On the top of each of them, a circular panel bore the gilt stamp of the British Crown. A few inches below it there was a gold hook.

Jack looked up at them and said, "Grinnies."

The man in the vest hung from the first grinny, strangled with a length of barbed wire. On the next pole, his wife dangled with a bullet hole in her forehead. The daughter was last. Someone had gutted her.

Jack ducked underneath the tank's turret gun and ran down the old road.

The corpse of an emaciated woman was on another grinny outside town. A poster beneath her body said, "H.M.

PLACEBO SECTOR 484. THIS CRIMINAL WAS EXECUTED FOR BREAKING THE CURFEW. GOD SAVE THE KING!"

Jack walked to the edge of the woods that overlooked the river.

Moonlight fell on the old town's ruined paper mill and derelict brewery, surrounded by rows of bombed-out shops and houses. He could see a checkpoint on the bridge but could not make out how many soldiers there were.

A searchlight shone on a man who was criss-crossing the wasteland by the river. Two soldiers were chasing him. Occasionally one stopped and fired a rifle.

The fugitive ran up the hill of bones and masonry. The soldiers followed their quarry.

Jack watched the soldiers and said, "I wouldn't bother. He's leading you into a trap."

A dull thud reverberated through the valley. The searchlight lit up an expanding ball of dark smoke. The soldiers lay motionless on the path.

Jack left the woods and picked his way through the ruined houses. Then he scrambled down the side of Badger's old bomb crater.

He searched in the debris. A piece of corrugated iron protruded from the dirt. He pulled it up.

A hand grabbed his leg and Jack fell through a hole onto a stone floor. A fist hit him in the teeth. Hands closed around his neck. He kicked his attacker and there was a grunt of pain.

Jack felt in his pocket and held up his lighter. The flame lit up a scarred face.

"You?" Badger said.

The fingers relaxed. He had stitched his cheek up. It made one eye look wider than the other.

"How did you get away, boy?"

"I was lucky."

Badger lit a candle.

There was an iron bed. A vase of snowdrops sat on a cabinet beside it. A piano stood in the corner of the room.

A leather sewing case lay beside a bloodstained porcelain jug on a dressing table.

"What do you think of the gaff?"

"I came here looking for your pistol," Jack said.

Badger pulled up an old wooden chair and sat on the bed.

He said, "Sit yourself down."

"We can't stay. There will be soldiers crawling all over the place in a minute."

Badger waved a hand at the chair. Jack sat down.

"They gave me two minutes. That was stupid—pretending to be sportsmen," he said.

Badger grinned and then winced, holding a hand to his cheek.

He said, "I had one chance. When the horseman came I jumped up high and grabbed him. We both fell. Then we both got up. So I punched him. Then I took his silly sword and his stupid white hat and his watch that he gave me two minutes on."

"Badger…"

"I put my good leg in the stirrup and hoisted myself up. I swear the nag knew who I was - or what I was up to. He shot off like a bullet. The other two chaps came after us and started shooting their little pistols. The dogs were yap yapping. The wind was whistling past and I thought—I'm beating them."

"The nag did all the work. If we needed to jump, he jumped—he wasn't scared. And every now and then he threw his head back and looked in my eyes, like he wanted me to be pleased."

Jack said, "So where did you go?"

"The village where I grew up. They still had the old grinnies on the roads, those that hadn't fallen down. Some had skeletons on, grinning down over all these years."

"I went to the old airfield and stood under the cob tree by the control tower. I tried to eat the nuts like I had with my dad, but my mouth was too sore and full of blood. I tried a few of the hiding places—the cinema, the old abbey. Nothing, just rubble and trees."

"Maybe it was the stolen uniform but there wasn't a living soul anywhere. You could feel it, no one was watching."

The lamp hissed softly.

"We should get out of here," Jack said.

"Suddenly I saw my own death. I was in some muddy dugout choking my guts out and trying to get a nice breath. Alone. Like always."

A tear rolled into the stitches on his cheek.

"You're not the first," he said.

"What?"

"The first person I did the dirty on."

Jack looked at the stone floor.

"There's no one left out there. King Eustace has won."

"I need to get into town before it gets light. Will you help me?"

The man thought for a moment and shook Jack's hand.

They climbed up the side of the crater. A searchlight swept across the ruined wasteland.

"Make for the trees," Badger said.

They ran. Then the light found Badger. For a second it bathed his thin body in white light. He stuck two-fingers up.

Several rifles fired at once. He fell forward. Cheering and whistling came from the riverbank. Jack ran into the tree line.

Leaves rustled. Moonlight fell on Badger's scarred face.

Jack said, "I thought they got you."

"Nah. I had it planned out. There's this little ditch I crawled up so they wouldn't see."

The horse had a blaze of white running over the ridge of his nose. Jack patted the animal's neck.

Badger pulled some clothes out of a saddlebag then threw the saddle over the horse.

He slung the blue cape around his shoulders and pulled the peak of the white helmet down to his nose. Then he threw out his chest and gave a smart salute.

Badger said, "This will fool them on the bridge. No mucking about."

"It's crawling with soldiers. What about swimming for it?"

"It's mined."

"I fish in it. We might be able to make it across."

"Come on, let's get moving. It doesn't matter how many are on the bridge. If they rumble us, we've had it anyway. Just lay over the back of the saddle like you're dead and I'll do the talking."

He led them out of the trees and they trotted down a path beside the hill.

"The Curfews are more scared of their officers than us. My Grandpa was in the real army before the Catastrophe. He did all the voices. He made us laugh," Badger said.

They rode to the bridge.

"Good evening, sir," a polite voice said.

Badger said, "I saw a cigarette on my way here. You could have given your position away."

The polite voice said, "I'm sorry, sir. I will find out who is responsible. May I see your papers please?"

"I'm not in the mood for any damn nonsense this evening. Stand aside."

"May I ask why you aren't wearing your riding boots sir?"

"What business is that of yours?"

"Would you mind getting down off your horse?"

Two shots were fired. Jack looked up. Badger had a smoking Webley in his hand. A pair of soldiers lay on the road. The others had run for cover.

They galloped across the old bridge into town.

A volley of shots followed them up the high street. The horse raced past a long row of burned-out shops and a decapitated statue of Queen Victoria.

Jack climbed up into the saddle and said, "You all right?"

Badger's eyes were half open. His eyeballs had rolled back. The stolen cape was soaked with blood.

Soldiers ran up the hill. Jack slid off the leather seat and rolled over the pavement into a patch of weeds.

Badger's body galloped up the road to London.

A voice said, "Over there."

Jack sprinted past a rotting bandstand. Rifles fired. He ducked into the derelict railway station and crossed over the tracks.

A poster had been nailed to the wall outside. There was a blurred picture of a man. Writing underneath said, "PROFESSOR DAVID CUNNINGHAM, THE SO-CALLED 'MEDICINE MAN' WANTED FOR ENCOURAGING APOCRYPHAL SICKNESS BELIEFS. EXECUTIONS IN THIS ZONE WILL CEASE UPON HIS CAPTURE OR DEATH."

Jack ripped it down.

The grey walls of the jail jutted over the east of the town. There were lights in the jailyard.

He ran up an alley that was choked with willow herb and emerged in an overgrown square.

Weeds grew between the cobbles.

There was a ragstone church. The grey building had a broken spire that now lay in three pieces on the ground.

He ran up a flight of stone steps to an arched doorway and went inside.

Chapter Three
The Medicine Man

A hexagonal stone font lay on the floor by the entrance.

The branches of yew trees had broken through a vaulted wooden ceiling and their leafless limbs filled the stone room.

Jack pushed his way through to an arched doorway.

A set of steps went down to a dark room full of plaques and inscriptions.

He stopped in front of a black sarcophagus. Letters carved into the side said, "HERE ETERNALLY LYETH DOCTORE W.W."

There was a length of old sacking hanging across a wall.

It covered the entrance to a long brick passageway.

He walked into a thirty-foot-wide spherical cave that had been carved out of grey ragstone.

The room had six brick tunnels leading off it.

A skylight let in some sunshine. It fell on a round table in the middle of the cave.

An old man wearing a green tunic slept with his head on the dusty surface.

He had a long beard and silver hair that hung down to his waist.

A young woman looked up from a map and said, "Look who's back."

Jack said, "Hello Bebo. Morning Grandpa."

The old man opened his eyes and smiled.

"We wanted to look for you but it was felt we couldn't give our position away," he said.

"I understand."

Jack pulled the poster out of his pocket and placed it on the table.

The old man read it.

"The Medicine Man. So it's me they're after."

"It looks that way," Jack said.

A young man came out of a tunnel and walked over to the table. He was a few years older than Jack. His hair was oiled and he had a pencil-thin moustache. There was a polished pistol holster on his hip.

He said, "You shouldn't have come back to the 'O'. You might have been followed."

"Nice to see you too, Jonathan."

Jonathan picked up the poster and said, "I don't know why they're bothering with you, Grandpa. It's not as if you've actually done anything for years."

Bebo said, "Jonathan and I have decided we're going to join up with the Resistance in the Essex badlands."

"If they still exist," Jack said.

"Well it's better than being a coward and doing nothing down here," Jonathan said.

The Medicine Man stood up.

He said, "Jack, you've got some blood on your face. Come on, let's get you cleaned up."

Jack followed the old man up one of the tunnels. They went into a little room lined with medicine cabinets whose shelves were filled with jars of pills.

There was a red cross on the wall. Black lettering beneath it said, "MEDICINE IS FREEDOM."

Jack sat in an old dentist's chair.

The Medicine Man soaked a flannel and wiped the boy's face.

He said, "I don't think your brother Jonathan is very pleased with us."

"Mum died on this seat. She said, 'Let the comfort come, let it rain on me.'"

"I remember."

"Why did you never tell us things, Grandpa?"

"In intelligence work it's sometimes best not to know, for your own protection."

"Do you think we are the only Resistance left now?"

"Perhaps. I don't know."

Jack took a connecting tunnel to the bathroom. He ran a bath and lowered himself into the hot water.

When he woke, the skylight was dark. He put on his trousers and ran upstairs.

The Medicine Man stood by the doorway. A hot breeze blew into the church.

Jonathan ran in. His face was covered in soot.

He said, "We went out. They're torching the town—house by house."

Bebo's blackened face was streaked with tears.

She said, "Why are they here?"

"It means a brave man has been captured," the Medicine Man said,

Jonathan said, "Who?"

"Chapman. He's the only one who knew the truth about this place."

A smoldering pigeon swooped through the entrance and skidded over the stone floor.

"I remember Chapman. He was always smiling," Bebo said.

"I have something they want. Something I should have destroyed years ago," the Medicine Man said

An explosion in the town rocked the church. The old man lost his footing and fell onto the floor. Jack helped him to his feet.

Jonathan said, "We're leaving, now!"

Jack went down to the dormitory. There was a long row of beds. Only two were made up.

Doctor Haverford-Granger lay in one of them, asleep. His white hair was fanned out over the pillow.

Jack shook him.

"Doctor, you have to get up. The ferrets are coming. Even the Medicine Man is leaving. Did you hear me? Professor Cunningham is leaving. You can't stay here."

The old man did not open his eyes.

Jack went up to the 'O.' Bebo and Jonathan were wearing khaki battle dress and light blue berets.

Jack said, "Why are you got up like that?"

"We're going to steal a tank," Bebo said.

She held up a thick green file. The front page said, "CENTURION BATTLE TANK, AUTOMOTIVE SYSTEMS."

"We've been practicing," Jonathan said.

He mimed steering the imaginary vehicle with two broom handles.

Bebo said, "We watched the jail this morning. There are tanks going in and out all the time."

Jonathan said, "They're not expecting any trouble."

Orange light flickered through the skylight window.

The young man looked up and said, "Ferrets. Time we were off."

The Medicine Man emerged from one of the tunnels. He looked more like the Professor Cunningham in the wanted poster. He had cut his hair and shaved his beard. His lined face looked small and pale under a trilby hat. His dark eyes were joyless. He wore a crumpled double-breasted suit and carried a scuffed leather satchel in a bony hand.

Jonathan said, "We are going to join the Resistance in Essex. Are you coming with us?"

"There's something I need to show you first."

"No time. They're here. What about you, Jack?"

"I want to see what grandpa has to show us."

Jonathan took Bebo's arm and pulled her away.

The Medicine Man said, "Goodbye then, and my blessings on the both of you."

Jack followed his grandfather into a narrow room lined with old files. The Medicine Man pulled a dummy metal bookcase that swung outwards on a hinge. It revealed a hidden doorway.

They went down a ragstone staircase.

The Medicine Man flicked a switch on the wall. A fluorescent light flickered on and lit up a ring of scuffed metal cabinets.

A three-foot-high stone column stood in the centre of the machines. It had grooves down the side.

A shallow purple bowl rested on top of it.

The Medicine man walked around the room flicking switches.

The cabinets were covered in glass displays and dials. Some contained rows of glass valves hanging off wooden racks. Everything was connected by masses of braided wire.

The Medicine Man pulled a sliding tray out of a cabinet. It had a typewriter on it. Behind the keys, there was a wooden back-board with coin-sized symbols.

He typed a few letters. The symbols lit up each time he pressed a key.

A delicate hammering noise came from a small black box beside the keyboard. A thin ribbon of perforated paper emerged out of it.

The Medicine Man said, "Co-ordinates."

Then walked to the centre of the room and knelt beside the column.

He ran his finger over a 2-inch metal band at the top of the stone plinth and the bowl. It had a vertical slot that he fed the paper into.

The metal band rotated the purple bowl a few degrees counter-clockwise.

The Medicine Man opened his satchel and took out a field mouse.

He placed the little animal in the bowl and said, "Sorry old boy."

The device made a tuneless humming sound.

The mouse tried to run but an unseen force held it in place.

The Medicine Man said, "Here we go."

The animal twisted suddenly as if it was wrung by invisible hands. Then the little body spun until the skin broke open and blood spattered over the bowl. The mouse's fur retreated into the pink flesh beneath it. The glistening tissue wound around itself and elongated until it became a pink string that rose upwards to form a half-circle above the purple vessel.

The Medicine Man said, "For some reason the cells need to be alive for the machine to work."

A moist film formed between the arched string of flesh and the bowl. A dark reflection of the room appeared in it.

Jack waved a hand. The gesture was echoed back at them.

He said, "Something about the reflection doesn't look right."

"It isn't a reflection. They are two people, like us."

"I don't understand."

"This machine is a doorway between worlds."

"They're in another world?"

"Yes. Very close to us on the spectrum. Practically identical to ours."

The membrane bulged briefly. For a second Jack caught the other Jack's eye.

He said, "Is the machine alive? I feel like it's looking at us."

"It certainly acts as a kind of observer. That's important, because you need an observer to get a different outcome."

"What do you mean?"

"Professor Singh had a theory—based on sub-atomic behavior—of how an elementary particle could exist as both a wave or a particle at the same time. Wave and particle exist in a superposition of two states—until they are measured and found to be in just one—when their wave function collapses. Theoretically, the earlier dual state would only be possible if the universe actually splits in two to accommodate both realities—wave or particle. Singh thought tiny changes like this could ultimately affect decisions people have made as well. Different decisions, different outcomes, different universes. Places where the dinosaurs never died out or Eustace Champion was never King. This machine is able to somehow detect and access them—possibly from particles leaking between universes or background radiation."

The arch of flesh pulsated.

"This device has god-like power. Whoever designed it used brute-force and guesswork to get what they wanted. I suspect it was designed by a machine."

"Grandpa. We need to go. The ferrets will be here any second.

The Medicine Man turned to him and said, "This thing is responsible for the destruction of this country, the death of your parents, the countless murders and massacres."

"How?"

"It just appeared out of nowhere. A group of scientists under my leadership were tasked with making it work. Sadly, King Eustace was one of them. Back then he was just Eustace Champion, a mediocre psychologist."

"You knew the King?"

"We sent volunteers through the machine. They came back saying they felt changed. We used x-ray tomography and established the journey had made changes in their bodies - they had been broken down and reassembled. The volunteers said it was like going through a mouth—and being digested."

"Eustace Champion became obsessed with the bizarre idea that the changes in the volunteers were psychological and not physical. Apocryphal sickness beliefs he called them. People feeling sorry for themselves. I suspected he had been secretly travelling through the Mouth and it had affected him. He was taken off the project and he disappeared. We think he used another Mouth. He reappeared a few weeks later and began the Catastrophe."

"What did the volunteers see on the other side?"

"Just ruined buildings for miles around. Eustace must have travelled further. Explored more worlds."

Jack said, "Why didn't you try and do the same thing he did? You had the Mouth."

The Medicine Man shrugged and said, "We spent a lifetime struggling over this. Haverford-Grainger, Singh and I made a decision that we would never send anyone through that thing again."

"But it could have saved us."

"How? What would we do? Destroy our enemies like he did? That would be futile. The damage was already done."

"But we've lost."

"I thought we could create a life here. That things would get better. Today, for the first time, I realise how completely Eustace has triumphed."

The Medicine Man placed his fingertips on the moist membrane. The counterpart Medicine Man on the other side of the mouth did the same. Their fingertips touched.

The lights flickered.

"We should go," Jack said.

They heard a cry. Doctor Haverford-Granger stood in the doorway at the top of the stairs. He was wearing pyjamas. He ran down the stone steps and fell forwards onto the floor, knocking Jack over.

The Medicine Man said, "Giles, the destination is too close on the spectrum. This is just a test."

The old doctor got up and dove head first into the membrane.

Another Haverford-Granger came out of the other side. Their heads and torsos merged. Then the new thing split in half. A pulpy mass of flesh and muscle spattered onto the floor.

The Medicine Man said, "I'll have to reset the machine."

"Why?"

"Jack, what would you say if I wanted you to go through with me, now?"

"After what you've told me, I would say no. I would say stick to the decision you made years ago. You could end up doing more damage than King Eustace."

"I want you to go through it with me. The Mouth tends to exaggerate people's personalities but I think a good lad like you would be all right."

A voice said, "Hello, anyone home?"

A figure in a silver flameproof suit and helmet stood at the top of the stone steps. He had a fuel tank strapped to his back.

He pointed his flamethrower at the Medicine Man.

Jack said, "No!"

A stream of liquid flame the colour of blood and gold engulfed the old man. When the jet died away, he fell backwards, knocking the Mouth over. The purple bowl skidded across the floor.

Smoke filled the room. Machinery blazed. The ferret pointed his flamethrower at Jack. A gun fired.

The man fell forward and slid down the stairs.

Jonathan walked through the doorway.

Jack knelt by the Medicine Man's charred body. The remains of his trilby had fused with his head. His lips moved.

He said, "The witch at Bromley."

Jonathan put his gun against the old man's left temple and pulled the trigger.

Chapter Four
The Cordon Sanitaire

Dark smoke wafted out of the tunnels and collected in the 'O'.

Jonathan said, "No ferrets. Come on."

They ran up a brick passageway into a little concrete room that smelt of alcohol.

They stopped in front of an old LISTER electrical generator whose spinning engine wheel was making a loud rattling noise. The late doctor Singh had converted it to run on distilled potatoes.

Jack said, "Why did you come back?"

"It wasn't my idea."

Jonathan pointed upwards. Bebo stared down at them through the room's open skylight.

Jonathan said, "You first."

Jack placed his boot on the fuel barrel of the machine and manhandled himself through the window.

Fog hung between the yew trees in an old graveyard.

Bebo said, "Where's the Professor?"

Jonathan got out and said, "Dead."

Bebo dropped a bundle of khaki clothes at Jack's feet.

Jonathan broke his Webley open and checked the chamber.

Jack put the enemy uniform on. It smelt of putrefaction.

Jonathan hoisted a canvas bag over his shoulder and said, "Come on then."

They climbed over the low ragstone wall at the back of the graveyard.

A light rain darkened the powdery grey ash that was falling on the road. The smog was so thick they could only see the broken tarmac a few feet ahead of them.

Soon the high prison walls loomed overhead.

Jonathan said, "They are using the back gates, so we'll use the old side entrance."

Bebo took out a box of *Players Navy Cut* and lit two cigarettes.

Jack said, "I'm not going."

The young woman said, "Don't be stupid. Where will you stay?"

"On the farm."

Jonathan said, "You can forget about that. We released the animals and burnt it yesterday. Wouldn't want the Royal Curfews enjoying it. Come on."

They stopped by the arched entrance. A sign overhead said, "H.M. PRISON MAIDSTONE". The door was rotten. Jonathan kicked it until the wood splintered.

They passed some upturned desks and walked through the cavernous building that had once held the prisoners. Nettle and Feverwort grew out of cracks in the stone floor.

In the prison yard acrid smog hung over a row of newly erected canvas tents.

Three Centurion tanks were silhouetted in the pale rectangle of an open prison gate.

A group of officers were gathered around a wooden trestle table studying a map. One of them was Prince Augustine Champion.

Behind them two mechanics worked on the engine of a Centurion.

Jonathan said, "We'll take the one nearest the gate. Jack, you follow Bebo. Any questions?"

They strolled across the yard. No one looked up.

Bebo walked behind the Centurion and swung her legs over the engine deck. Jack followed her. Jonathan climbed up onto the front hull and opened the driver's hatch. Bebo got into the turret.

The cabin smelled of cordite and old sweat. Jack squeezed into a leather chair below Bebo. His knees touched the metal loading hatch of the 16-pounder.

The engine gunned. The stolen tank did a stationary pivot towards the vehicle gate.

The officers looked up from the map.

Bebo pushed a radio headset over Jack's ears.

She said. "I need an armour-piercing shell."

She pointed to a storage hatch. Jack took out a long torpedo-shaped shell and pushed it into the breach of the big gun.

Bebo touched the instrument panel. The turret swung towards the nearest Centurion.

Jack looked through his periscope. The two mechanics were waving their hands.

A dark-haired officer drew his revolver and fired a shot in the air. Jonathan laughed.

The tank fired. The shell hit the Centurion low down. A ball of flame and shrapnel swept out from beneath the vehicle's belly as it flipped half over and then righted itself with a crash.

Jonathan said, "Good shot."

The gun rotated towards the third war machine. Jack ejected the smoking shell and dropped it into a canvas bin beside his seat. He shoved a new missile into the breach.

The long gun fired again. The side of the third tank exploded in flames and it skidded across the courtyard into the prison wall.

The stolen Centurion roared through the prison gates into town.

Jonathan said, "That wiped the smile off their faces. I hope we got Augustine."

Jack looked into his periscope. They were on the arterial road that wound through the shattered suburbs. Silver-suited ferrets were burning terraced houses.

"According to the gauge she's got enough diesel to get us to bandit country," Jonathan said.

Ruined houses gave way to fields.

Bebo said, "Checkpoint."

The tank lurched to a halt.

There were some looted wooden dining chairs by the side of the road. Two seated Curfew soldiers shouted encouragement to a shaven-headed comrade who was thumping an old man in the face.

An officer read a copy of *The Daily Truth*.

A woman lay dead in the long grass.

Bebo got down beside Jack and put the wooden stock of the Centurion's 50 millimetre machine-gun against her shoulder. She stared into the gun sight.

The officer stood up and looked at them with a pair of binoculars.

Bebo squeezed the trigger.

The man's head exploded in a pink mist.

The other soldiers ran for cover in the bushes. Bebo got two of them before they made it.

The stolen war machine pushed on into the Weald. The winter sun cast a pale light over abandoned fields.

After a few minutes Bebo said, "We're coming to the Cordon Sanitaire. The map says the Resistance breach is a quarter of a mile east of here."

Jonathan turned the vehicle into an overgrown field, letting out whoops of triumph when he knocked over a tree or an old hop pole.

Then Bebo said, "This is it."

They climbed out of the Centurion and stood in silence. Rusting vehicles were strewn across the landscape ahead of them.

Clumps of thorn and sycamore grew amongst lines of abandoned civilian cars.

There were patches of brown earth where detonator acid from old Hedgehog area-denial mines had leaked into the soil.

Ahead of them an unmanned light aircraft was buried in the earth, nose first. Underneath a crust of flaking white paint, the wings were the same purple as the Mouth.

Jonathan pointed to a burned-out tank that was covered in creepers.

He said, "That's a Pershing from the American expedition."

Bebo positioned a compass over her map.

She said, "Everything is so overgrown. I can't see any of the wrecked vehicles they use for markers."

Jonathan disappeared into the Centurion and re-emerged with a wooden crate. It had ROYAL CURFEW REGIMENT MINE DETECTOR stencilled on the side.

He screwed a flat circular head onto a telescopic grip.

"The mines are all sixty years old now so hopefully they're duff," he said.

They took turns sweeping a tank-sized lane. By the late afternoon they had found two mines and marked them with the used shells.

Jack waved the device over some long grass. Jonathan tapped his shoulder.

"It's getting dark. We're going to have to risk going over in the tank," he said.

Jonathan and Bebo walked back. Jack relaxed his arm and the metal head of the detector touched a frozen clod of earth. An orange light bit into his eyes. A force plucked him high into the air, and he fell into darkness.

He woke sitting in the fighting compartment. The tank was on the move over rough ground. Bebo was bandaging his hand. She slid the headphones over his ears.

"The good news is I packed some of your grandpas's supplies."

She held up an old canvas shoulder bag with a red cross on it and letters underneath that said MEDICINE IS FREEDOM.

"The bad news is you've lost a finger. Shrapnel. Sorry. You're lucky you didn't die."

Beneath the layers of a square field dressing, he felt a pain where his index finger was severed below the second knuckle.

Bebo said, "I sewed your finger up."

She shook a pill out of a glass bottle and pushed it into his mouth.

She said, "Antibiotics. King Eustace wouldn't approve."

She held a water bottle up to his lips.

Jack said, "Stop the tank. Let me out."

"It's too late. We're nearly across."

Bebo broke the cap off a syrette of morphine.

"A last present from the Medicine Man."

The needle pricked Jack's skin and the contents of the collapsible tube went into his stomach.

Jonathan said, "We're through."

The old road through the woods resumed.

The wall around London was silhouetted on the horizon.

Old grinnies were dotted along the road on both sides.

Jonathan said, "Bastards."

Bebo said, "There's an old Resistance farm marked on the map near here."

They turned up a pot-holed dirt track. Jack closed his eyes and fell asleep.

Later he opened the hatch and got out.

The war machine was parked in a concrete yard between two derelict barns.

He jumped down and winced at the pain in his hand.

Jonathan and Bebo had chosen a space in a ruined stable that was sheltered by a section of roof.

They sat around a fire and ate stolen rations.

Jack stared up at the roof beams and said, "What's next?"

His brother sucked a boiled sweet.

"We're going to bring London to its knees," he said.

"On your own?"

Jonathan looked at Jack through the fire.

He said, "There hasn't been an uprising in twenty years. They aren't expecting trouble."

"The people in London are brainwashed. They don't want to be saved by you and they won't thank you."

"Dad was nailed up to a grinny for fighting King Eustace. He would be ashamed of you. What do you suggest we should do then?"

"I don't know. The only way we can beat him is to stay civilised."

"How do we do that?"

"We were managing it until yesterday."

They stared at the fire for a while.

Bebo said, "We are going to find the Resistance in Essex. Then we will bomb London into submission and nail King Weasel up on a grinny. Or die trying."

"There no-one left in Essex," Jack said.

"Then we'll do it ourselves," she said.

Jack unbuttoned the front of his tunic and took out the purple bowl.

He said, "Grandpa showed me this incredible device."

Bebo said, "What is it?"

"It creates a doorway into another world. I saw it working. Doctor Haverford-Grainger went through it. Eustace Champion used one to take over."

He handed the receptacle to Bebo.

Jonathan said, "If it's so incredible why didn't Grandpa use the machine himself?"

"He thought it would do more harm than good."

"Typical."

Jonathan took the bowl and ran his fingertips over the rim.

Jack said, "Grandpa thought we could find someone who could make it work. In Bromley."

Jonathan considered for a minute and shook his head.

"It's a bit pie-in-the-sky. Anyway Bromley is too near the wall."

"Sorry, Jack," Bebo said.

They took camp beds from the tank and set them up around the fire.

Jonathan hung a long piece of cord around the ruined barn and tied the ends together, dangling two empty cans from the knot.

They clinked just before the dawn. Jack half-opened an eyelid. There were two shadows in the stables. They wore animal skins and had a faint smell of sweat and excrement.

The older of the two had white hair and dark skin. She had smallpox scars on her cheeks. The younger one had a long beard and shaved head. The woman made a sign and they retreated into the night.

At daybreak, a grey mist had settled over the ruined courtyard.

Jack heard the Centurion pulling out of the yard.

Then he heard another engine. The noise was lower-pitched and came from the sky.

He ran along the pot-holed track.

A bug-shaped helicopter hovered over the road a mile away.

He could not see the Centurion but heard the vehicle's 50mm machine gun.

A few seconds later, there were two whistling noises and a booming explosion.

The helicopter hovered for a few seconds. Then it banked and flew towards Jack.

Chapter Five
The Last Resistance Fighter

$\mathcal{E}$ach step on the frozen ground sent a jolt of pain through his body.

The flying machine appeared above the bare branches in the tree canopy.

Jack heard a high-powered rifle shot. A bullet hole disfigured the smooth bark of a nearby beech tree.

The cabin of the helicopter was open. The sniper's long legs dangled over the side of the hovering vehicle.

Dead leaves whirled in the air.

The gunman looked through his telescopic sight and pulled the trigger. Jack was knocked off his feet.

The sniper shouted something to the pilot. The helicopter circled back towards the farm.

A figure ran out from behind a tree and knelt beside him. He looked up and saw the silver-haired woman from the night before.

They both stared at a hole in the front of his tunic. Jack pulled the garment up. There was no blood. The purple bowl had stopped the bullet.

The old woman said, "The snatch squad will come back on foot."

Jack stood up and then fell to his knees.

"I'm too sick," he said.

She put her arms around his waist. They broke into a shambling run.

Helicopter rotors powered down in the distance.

They fled through woodland pastures until Jack lost his footing and slid down the side of a shallow brook. He lay on the bank and retched a few times.

"Leave me," he said.

The old woman hoisted him over her shoulders.

Jack woke up propped against a wall of damp earth. A thin stream of water trickled down the nape of his neck and over his arm. He nodded off again.

A voice next to his ear said, "Better stop snoring, the brainwash boys will hear you."

He straightened up.

The total darkness was indistinguishable from unconsciousness.

A hand shook his shoulder. A square of moonlight opened above his head. Some leaves fell from above. Soft rain fell on his face.

The old thief climbed up a wooden ladder.

Then she looked down on him and said, "Why are they after you?"

"We stole a tank."

The woman laughed and said, "What's your name?"

"Jack."

"I'm Noel."

Jack climbed out of the hole. He felt a wave of illness pass through his body and it went dark.

He woke up wrapped in a warm animal skin. Daylight shone through a small opening in a rock wall. The floor was paved with dark flint. He could smell cooking. The old woman put a pill in his mouth and made him drink. Then she pushed a syrette needle into his stomach and squeezed out a dose of morphine.

That night a dog lay on the floor beside the bed. His dreams were filled with unwanted memories.

The next day he heard a conversation in another room.

A male voice said, "They sent a helicopter. That means he's valuable. We could hand him in. They pay good money for escapees."

Noel said, "You're too young to remember the behavioural camp. If you did, you wouldn't talk like that."

Jack closed his eyes.

When he woke again a setting sun shone through the opening in the rock.

The old woman sat at a wooden table with a young man. He had a shaved head and long beard. They were eating stew.

Jack sat up.

Noel said, "Ah Jack, this is my son Roland."

She gestured at the man. He did not look up from his meal.

Jack said, "Thank you for looking after me. I just want to go to Bromley."

Roland said, "No-one just wants to go to Bromley. It's too dangerous. What is your business there?"

"You wouldn't believe me."

The old woman said, "Try us."

"I have information that could lead to the defeat of King Eustace and his illegal regime."

Roland laughed loudly.

He said, "Great. You've saved a lunatic."

Noel said, "Lie down and get some rest."

Jack lay back on his bed and closed his eyes.

Later that night a hand gently shook his shoulder. Noel crouched beside him. She had a tallow candle in her hand. The flickering light threw her smallpox scars into relief.

She put a finger to her lips and placed a bundle of oil-stained rags on the floor.

"Roland wouldn't like it if he knew I was talking to you."

She unwrapped the bundle and held up a rusty tin whose label said, BOURNVILLE COCOA.

"Know what this is?"

Jack shook his head.

"Tin grenade. Old now. Bloody effective in its time, though."

Noel pulled a machine gun from the rags. The snub-nosed barrel had a perforated metal jacket.

She slotted a magazine into the side of the weapon and said, "I was in the Walthamstow Brigade, in the uprisings. I served under Joshua Hooper, you heard of him?"

"Who hasn't?"

"This gun saw some action. Vicious bit of tin. Do you know what it is?"

"It's a Sten gun."

"The weapon of the Resistance. Helped make this one myself. Good for close quarters. Used to seize up if the weather was bad."

Noel handed the gun to Jack. It was cold and heavy.

Jack said, "My trigger finger was blown off by a mine."

"So you're going after King Eustace?"

"I hope so."

"He always had the jump on us. Unmanned aircraft was the rumour. Most of us were killed or taken for behavioural modification."

"You were in the camps?"

"I was one of the majority who didn't respond to therapy. After a while if you didn't agree with King Eustace's beliefs the brainwash boys beat you to death. I saw that a lot. They killed my husband. I found my boy and got out. We were the only ones to ever make it out of a Gold-Standard Behavioural Unit. We got through the gates in the boot of the Commandant's car."

Jack handed the gun back and said, "Good for you."

Noel reached into her bundle and held up a handful of 9mm bullets.

"This was a great country. I am Resistance, and proud. We landed some hard blows when we could."

"I'm sure you did."

"Take me with you. My son doesn't remember when we fought back. But I do."

Jack shook his head and said, "I can't."

Noel said, "All my life I've waited for the war criminals to be put on trial and punished—King Eustace Champion, Audley, all of them. Now I realize they will just get off scot-free."

She carefully wrapped up the bundle.

Jack said, "My Dad was Resistance."

"Did he see much action?"

"Kent uprising."

"I'm worried about Roland. I think you should leave here as quickly as you can."

She stood up, gave a mock military salute and blew the candle out.

An hour before sunrise Jack put his khaki uniform back on. Noel had left him an animal skin waistcoat with a furry collar. The medical bag and the bowl lay on the floor beside a jar with two pickled eggs in it.

A ragstone corridor led to an oak front door. He went out onto a stone terrace. The little clearing was fringed with rhododendron.

There was a wooden hatch in the centre of the stones.

It covered a dark hole that smelled of earth.

He jumped down and landed on a wooden platform whose wheels squeaked.

The tunnel was only three feet high. There was a rope overhead. He lay down and pulled on it with his good hand. The little vehicle began to move.

The track went on for a while.

He climbed out into the forest and followed a track that went north.

Roland sat on the gnarled trunk of a fallen ash tree.

He said, "It's a few miles to Bromley. It's easy to get lost around here. I'll take you there."

There was an axe in his hand.

Jack said, "I'll be fine."

Roland stood up and walked over to him.

"The old woman is weak. I'm not," he said.

Noel walked up the path. She had a roe deer over her shoulders.

She said, "We're all up nice and early."

Roland said, "I'm taking him to Bromley."

"He can find his own way there."

"He could lead them straight to us."

"He's a good lad, he wouldn't do that. Off you go, boy."

Jack jogged up the path. Roland came after him and grabbed his legs. They fell onto the ground. Roland raised his axe into the air.

Noel grabbed her son's wrist. Jack struggled out from underneath them.

He ran up the path and then zigzagged through the trees until he came to the edge of the forest and his legs collapsed underneath him.

Chapter Six
A Bit of Luck

*H*e rolled down a muddy bank into a fast-flowing river of sewage.

The cold brown water swept him downriver. He caught hold of an exposed tree root and climbed back onto the land, lying still for a while.

Further up he found an ash tree that had fallen across the water and made a bridge.

On the other side, there was a hill of rotting clothes and rusty barrels. The tubs leaked foul-smelling chemicals.

A pair of crows circled overhead.

Rats skirted a pool of viscous water.

The cold wind carried a sweet fetid smell.

A pair of legs protruded from a rectangular trench of dirty ice.

A stray mongrel ran past him.

He spent an hour walking the paths that ran between mountains of waste.

Then Bromley was spread out in front of him—thousands of shacks sitting on acres of dark earth.

The bomb-damaged municipal buildings of the old town made a line on the horizon.

Jack sat on a metal barrel that said USE YOUR CHEM MASK FOR EVERY TASK.

He ate a pickled egg while the sun lowered in the sky.

At twilight a siren sounded. The alleys filled with ragged men and women returning from work.

Oil lamps were lit inside the huts and flickered behind shuttered windows.

In a few minutes, thousands of cooking fires left a smoke haze over the moon.

When it was night, Jack took a churned-up mud track into the shantytown.

A thin man with wiry hair stood in the doorway of a shack. He held a rolled-up cigarette between his finger and his thumb.

Jack stopped and said, "Good evening. I wonder if you could help me? I'm trying to find someone."

"Cough cough, do you mind if I stand here and have a quiet fag without you asking me silly bugger questions?"

"Have you heard of someone called the Witch of Bromley?"

"Cough cough, cough cough, get lost!"

A tall woman with greasy hair stepped out onto the front porch of the next hut and threw a half brick. It bounced off Jack's head. He slipped and fell backwards into the mud.

She said, "We don't like riff-raff and gypsies around here."

Jack got up and continued along the track to a muddy crossroads.

The body of a naked middle-aged man hung from a grinny. A sign around his neck said, THIS MAN DIED OF CANCER BECAUSE HE FAILED NEUROPSYCHOLOGICAL RE-EDUCATION. DO NOT FAIL YOUR TREATMENT. GOD SAVE THE KING!

There was a faded poster of King Eustace beneath the body. He was wearing a white suit and looking down from the clouds. There was the usual small smile of pretend modesty.

Jack walked towards the old town. The path terminated suddenly in a padlocked gate.

A sign said, RECREATION GROUND, ACCESS FORBIDDEN DURING EVENING CURFEW.

He climbed over a chain-link fence and followed a muddy path between two overgrown meadows.

There was a clearing with a statue of King Eustace shouting into a loud hailer and waving a fist. An inscription on a marble plinth said, KING, VISIONARY, QUACK-KILLER "A FELLOW OF GENIUS"

Jack thought for a moment and then spat on it.

Someone in the distance shouted, "Oi!"

He ran into the meadow and fought through a mass of tall wildflowers.

Jack emerged onto an immaculate lawn and saw the silhouette of a large building ahead of him.

A sign said, THE ROOKERY—PSYCHONEUROLOGICAL UNIT.

A wooden bridge spanned a frozen pond.

He ran over it and crouched beside a privet hedge.

The building ahead of him was covered in ivy. Electric light spilled out of tall windows onto a gravel forecourt.

Two nurses smoked beside the entrance. A man walked out of the reception hall and joined them. He wore a red leather holster over a white lab coat. The man lit a cigarette and said something. All three of them laughed.

Jack heard a groan. A pale fair-haired man lay on the lawn a few feet in front of him. He was wearing a surgical gown.

The smokers ground their cigarette butts into the gravel and went inside the house.

Jack crawled over and said, "Are you alive?"

The patient groaned. There was a bullet hole in his thigh. The grass underneath it was dark with blood.

He opened his eyes and said, "Who are you?"

Jack unwrapped the bandage from his hand and wound it around the man's leg.

He said, "Nobody. Look, I'm looking for someone. Have you heard of the Witch of Bromley?"

The wounded man thought and said, "I could take you to someone who might know."

Jack picked the patient up in his arms.

The man with the red holster raced out of the entrance and shouted, "Stop!"

An alarm went off.

Jack ran over the bridge and fought through the meadow. He lowered the patient over the fence and carried him into the shantytown.

The wounded man said, "Here. Opposite the water pump."

Jack pushed a corrugated iron door open.

The house had a mud floor and cardboard in the windows.

An old couple sat on two chairs in the front room.

Jack went into the back room and laid the patient on a mattress.

The old woman felt the young man's neck for a pulse. She bowed her head and let out a cry of anguish.

Jack said, "I'm sorry. I'm trying to find someone."

"Who?"

"Someone called the The Witch of Bromley."

The woman wiped tears from her eyes and said, "Who are you?"

"I'm nobody. Please, it's very important."

The man pulled an old leather bible from underneath the bed's mattress. He ripped out the back page and quickly sketched a map with a stub of pencil.

When it was finished he handed it to Jack.

He pointed to the letter 'X' at the top and said, "I heard the witch lived in the caves. The ferrets burned them out a long time ago."

Soldiers were banging on doors in the alley.

Jack picked the body up and pushed the back door open.

A row of muddy gardens took him into the mountainous wasteland.

He dropped the corpse in the stinking river and walked across the fallen tree into the dark forest.

The old man had drawn a railway line to the northeast. Half-an-hour later Jack found it.

He climbed over a metal fence and slid down steep sidings.

He walked along the tracks for a while. The rails made a rumbling noise and he hid under a bush. A long freight train sped past.

He came to a whitewashed railway station called PETTS WOOD.

The building was empty. A poster on the waiting room wall said, GOT YOUR VISA FOR THE PEACE WALL? UNAUTHORISED TRAVEL IS TREASON AND IS PUNISHABLE BY SUMMARY EXECUTION.

Jack walked out into a car park. He studied the map and turned into the forest. In a few minutes, he found the clearing the old man had drawn.

A sign saying, THIS WAY TO THE CAVES led to a stone courtyard at the foot of a raised plateau of grassland.

The arched entrance to the caves had been blown up. It was plugged with tons of limestone spoil.

A gust of cold rain wet the back of his head.

Patches of white chalk showed between the green scrub on the raised plateau over the caves.

He sat beneath a curved piece of white rock, swallowed an antibiotic and injected himself with the last of the morphine.

Then he watched the sun rise and enjoyed it.

The sound of a vehicle driving through the woods woke him.

A few yards to his right, a man with a haggard face ran through the bushes.

Jack said, "Hey, wait!"

An armoured jeep with ROYAL PROTECTION AGENCY written on its side stopped outside the blown-up entrance.

The man disappeared behind a clump of hawthorn bushes.

Two men in blue uniform got out of the jeep and let an Alsatian off the leash.

Jack saw the man disappear into a hole in the ground. He pulled up a crate lid covered with grass and turf.

A pale face looked up from the darkness.

The man said, "Get away from here."

"They'll kill me."

"I'll kill you."

Jack climbed into the hole. The man caught his legs and tried to push him back out. He lost his footing and they rolled together down a long gravel slide.

Chapter Seven
Amy

There was no light.

A hand grabbed Jack's hair. A blade pressed against his throat.

"I was sent by the Medicine Man."

"Stop talking."

The man was wheezing heavily. His breath smelled of alcohol.

Jack butted the back of his head into the man's nose. His attacker cried out and scrambled over the gravel.

He said, "This place is thousands of years old. There are hundreds of miles of passages. Without a map or a light you will die here. So go back up there. Don't follow me or I will kill you."

Footsteps ran down a tunnel.

Jack took out his grandfather's brass lighter.

The little flame illuminated a chalk passageway whose walls were striped with lines of dark flint.

He walked to a doorway which led into a square room. The carved-out chamber was half-filled with debris from a roof fall. He crawled over it to a passage on the other side that sloped downwards.

Further down the tunnel he tripped over a ridge in the floor and fell face first onto hard chalk. Cold water trickled over his fingers. It ran in a channel beside the path. He scooped up a handful. It tasted of iron and he spat it out.

The passage ended in a bottle-shaped room that smelled of corruption.

Jack held up his lighter. There was a long brick trough in the middle of the room. It had bulging white-capped mushrooms growing out of it. He pulled one out and ate it.

He had to stoop in the next tunnel. The ceiling grew steadily lower until he was crawling on hands and knees.

Then the passage stopped. He took out his lighter and the flame flickered in a draught of air that came from above him.

There was a narrow up-shaft. He squeezed into it. Flint pebbles scraped his rib cage. He moved up inch by inch, pushing with his feet and pulling with his good hand.

There was a square hole in the shaft. He climbed out onto a limestone floor.

The lighter lit up a long room with blackened walls. There was a line of half-melted metal bedsteads on one side.

On the end wall, a red cross painted on a white circle had survived the flamethrowers.

Boot leather creaked. Something hard and flat hit Jack on the back of his head. The force knocked him flat.

He rolled sideways to avoid a second blow. The weapon clanged on the floor.

Jack said, "There's no need for this. I'm just trying to find someone."

He heard heavy breathing.

Jack swung his feet in a circle and knocked the man's legs from underneath him. There was silence.

Jack lit his lighter.

The haggard man lay face down on the floor. He had a spade in one hand. Blood leaked from a gash in his forehead.

There was a paraffin lamp on the floor behind the body. Jack lit it.

A girl ran into the room. Her dark hair was braided in two plaits. She looked younger than Jack.

She said, "What have you done to Bill?"

"He was trying to kill me."

"Who are you? Are you a brainwash boy?"

"No."

"Then why are you wearing a Curfew uniform?"

"Long story. What's your name?"

She thought for a moment and said, "Amy. What's yours?"

"Jack."

He rubbed the back of his head and turned to his attacker. The haggard man was staring up at him.

Jack said, "I came here to look for someone. That's all. Then I will leave you alone."

Bill said, "There's no-one else here. It's just me and the girl."

"Do you know someone called the Witch of Bromley?"

Bill got up onto his elbows and winced.

"The Witch of Bromley wasn't a witch and she wasn't from Bromley, as far as I know," he said.

"Can I meet her?"

"She's been dead for many years."

"Who was she?"

"Her name was Professor Ann Soper, she worked for the Resistance. Witch was her code-name."

"Did she live down here?"

"A long time ago. Before the brainwash boys found this place."

"What happened to her?"

"Same as everyone else. Burned down here or shot by the Royal Curfews on the surface."

"They got everyone?"

"Except me."

"Did she keep any papers or a journal or something?"

Bill thought for a minute.

"I have a letter she wrote."

"Could I see it?"

"It's addressed to Professor David Cunningham."

"He was my grandfather."

Bill groaned and said, "I feel dizzy. I'm not sure I can move."

Amy said, "Wait."

They waited in silence.

There was a squeaking sound as she returned with a wheelbarrow.

Jack put his arms under Bill's shoulders and Amy took his legs. They lifted him into the little vehicle.

Amy wheeled the old man into a wide tunnel outside. Jack followed with the lamp. The passage was lined with abandoned shops. The carved-out rooms were blackened by fire. The writing on most of the wooden storefronts was burned.

Only a CANTEEN that had once offered LIGHT MEALS AND HOT DRINKS had escaped the fire.

They stopped outside. Amy helped Bill to his feet. They walked past some broken tables and a wooden counter.

A set of steps led to a battered metal door.

It opened into a room carved out of chalk. A working electric light hung from the ceiling.

There were framed photographs on the walls. One showed a young David Cunningham with his arm around a brunette woman.

A metal stove stood in the middle of a carved-out fireplace at the end of the room.

Amy helped the haggard man into an armchair.

The man said, "Do you have a name?"

"Jack."

"I'm Bill."

Bill held out his hand. Jack shook it.

Amy placed a kettle on the stove.

Bill said, "This was my dad's place. He was a big cheese in the Resistance."

Jack said, "Could I see the letter?"

Bill got up and opened a doorway into a side room.

Amy grabbed Jack's arm and said, "He is going to kill you. He kills anyone who comes here."

"What?"

"He murdered my Mum and Dad. I'm sure he did—I can't remember. I was too young."

Bill came out of the room. Amy went back to the stove.

The letter was addressed to THE MEDICINE MAN. The envelope had been opened.

Jack unfolded the paper and read,

"Station 62, June 1963.

My dear David,

Someone has betrayed our position to the enemy. A mobile fire unit is burning us out tunnel by tunnel. You may never read this but I want to write it.

No relationship ends elegantly but I look back at the time we were together, even the months after the catastrophe, as the happiest in my life—because I was with you.

You said you had destroyed the Mouth in station 60. I never for one second believed you. We assembled a Mouth here. We set up the computers and the column was easy to fabricate. But we could not copy the bowl, which, as you know, is a crystalline computer too complicated to reproduce.

We only had half a machine. We planned to take the bowl from you by force, if necessary, and give Britain a last chance.

This is the argument that drove us apart. David you must by now see that doing nothing will mean death for all of us.

I hope this letter reaches you my darling. I have thought of you every day throughout the long years.

With my love, Ann."

Jack said, "Is there a room in this place that's full of metal boxes and wires?"

Bill said, "How do you know about that?"

"I'd like to see it."

The kettle whistled. Amy took it off the stove.

Bill pointed to a bookcase on the right of the fireplace.

He said, "Through there. Give the right hand side a shove. Help yourself, young man."

The wooden shelves had a few old Resistance manuals with titles like THE SPOTTER'S GUIDE TO AERIAL WAR MACHINES. There was a fat book written by King Eustace called DEATH TO THE DOUBTERS.

Jack pushed the bookcase. It swung backwards.

The brick room behind it was smaller than its counterpart in the 'O'. The machinery looked newer. Rats had chewed the rubber insulation on the wires.

Bill appeared in the doorway and said, "The brainwash boys never found this place."

Jack said, "Does it have electricity?"

"No one has used it in the fifty years since it was set up."

"Do you know how any of this works, Bill?"

"Not a clue, mate."

Amy said, "He keeps it working. There is a generator."

Bill said, "Amy, go back to the house. I want to have a private conversation with our guest."

Jack flicked a switch on the cabinet that contained the cipher machine. Green lights flickered in two circular glass displays.

"It still works. Fancy that," said Bill.

Amy said, "You're not the first one who's come here looking for this. It's a trap."

Bill walked over to Amy and punched her in the face. She fell against one of the metal cabinets and slid down it onto the floor.

Bill turned to Jack and said, "Now look what you made me do."

"You're a traitor."

"It was that or get barbecued. I was just a boy."

Amy groaned.

Jack said, "Why did you come back here?"

"I was re-educated. They sent me back to do my patriotic duty against weaklings like you. I've got the George medal."

He tapped his breast. Something underneath his coat clinked.

"Does King Eustace know about this room?"

Bill gestured at Amy and said, "You made me do that."

He limped over to Jack.

Jack said, "Stay away from me."

The haggard man grabbed his throat. They both went down, with Bill on top. The man squeezed. Jack tried to push him away. The old man was too heavy and the grip was too strong.

Something shattered on the side of Bill's head. Paraffin ran into his eyes, catching fire a split-second later. Drops of it set fire to the fur collar on Jack's coat.

Bill got up onto his knees and tried to wipe the burning oil out of his eyes. Amy held up a spade and smashed it on the old man's head. Bill fell forward. Amy hit his head again.

She said, "He buries the bodies in the mulch we grow the mushrooms in. After I found the first one I worked out he must have killed mum and dad."

Jack walked over to the stone pedestal in the middle of the room. He took the bowl out and placed it on the little column.

She said, "What does it do?"

"It's a doorway to another world. But I don't know how to make it work."

"If I help you will you take me with you?"

There was a rusty document box beside one of the cabinets.

Amy pulled the top open. A heavy Mills bomb grenade fell out and rolled across the floor.

She said, "He never taught me to read. He said I wouldn't need to."

Jack leafed through a few sheets and selected a wad of yellowing type-written paper. The front page said,

"Operation of 'Station 62.' Most Secret. By WITCH. September 1958"

"CONFIDENTIAL. Description, Use of portable cipher machine with rotor-based scrambler to send, code, receive and decode messages from a counterpart universe cipher machine using background radiation.

Warning, During Phase I tests volunteers sustained physical trauma including myocardial infarction and brain injury.

Instructions, the following code has been gained by covert operations and is further up the spectrum than previous recorded missions. It contains position, date and time and must be entered for a successful link, Co-ordinates [a81/05/71] [68/9015]."

Amy said, "What does it say?"

Jack went to the cipher machine and typed the digits.

Symbols lit up on the wooden backboard.

A ribbon of hole-punched paper emerged out of a black box beside the keyboard. He fed the slot in the metal bracelet. The Mouth made clicking noises. The bowl rotated a few degrees.

Amy said, "I want to go with you."

"No. This thing is too dangerous. What comes out is not the same as what goes in."

"If this machine is so bad why are you using it?"

Jack dragged Bill over to the Mouth and said, "Because my grandfather asked me to. He made a mistake, and he knew it."

He propped Bill against a cabinet and placed the man's palm on the surface of the purple bowl.

The Mouth hummed. Bill's pudgy fingers began to twist around each other. He grunted. The splintered bones in the gyrating digits burst through the turning skin.

Then his whole arm revolved. The muscle and tissue spun around. A newly created tube of glistening matter separated itself from Bill's shoulder.

He slumped onto the floor.

The newborn thing twisted into a thick rope of arched flesh. A central bubble formed beneath it.

Through it, they could see the blurred outline of a white room.

Amy said, "Where is that?"

"I don't know. If I live I'll come back for you. I promise."

Jack arched his arms above his head and dived into the Mouth.

Part II: The New World

Chapter Eight
Pierre Wilson

A wave of fire ate into skin, muscle and bone. Parcels of time, each an evil season, were filled with different agonies. Sometimes they eased enough for him to recollect who and what he was. Finally, his physical body disappeared and he became a presence. There was just enough consciousness left to mutely witness what the mouth was doing—it was murdering him. Then he was gone and something else appeared.

Jack fell onto a black carpet. There was no rusting machinery but it looked like the room he had just left. There was a table and a screen on which the words EMERGENCY ACTIVATION blinked on and off.

The translucent film under the arch bulged and Amy fell onto him.

Jack said, "I told you not to come after me."

Amy rolled off him and said, "I was dead."

Jack held his hand up. A baby digit had burst through the stitched-up stump of his index finger. He wiggled it. It looked pink and new.

The arch above the Mouth collapsed. Pieces of Bill's flesh splattered over them.

A key turned in a door.

A man switched the light on. He had a round face and dark hair that was tied in a pony tail. His blue jumper had a badge that said, HILARY FAIRHURST — GOLD STANDARD SECURITY.

Jack and Amy pushed past him.

Hilary said, "You two smell like shit."

There were no burned-out shops here. Just a White tunnel with a red carpet. It terminated with a door that had GOLD STANDARD DEEP LEVEL DOCUMENT STORAGE written on it.

Hilary said, "There's no way out of here. Everything is locked down."

A plastic card hung from a blue ribbon around the security man's neck. He waved it over a matchbox-sized sensor.

The door opened into a wooden office. Three windows looked out onto a giant cave filled with cardboard document boxes.

A door on the right had a sensor.

Hilary picked up a telephone. He pressed a button and said, "This is Document Storage. I have detained the two trespassers."

Jack yanked the ribbon over the man's head. He waved the card in front of the sensor and took Amy's hand.

They ran between the stacked document boxes.

Amy said, "Over there."

She pointed to a lift with a latticed metal gate.

Amy slid the door to one side.

Jack said, "I read about these."

He pulled the door shut and pushed the button for UPPER LEVELS. The machine hummed and the metal cage moved upwards.

"What happened in the Mouth?" Amy said.

"Don't think about it."

"I'm not going back in that thing."

"You don't have to."

Jack pulled the lift doors open.

They ran past a wooden reception desk, through the front door and into the night.

Lampposts cast circles of light over a tarmac expanse.

There was a single red van with a logo that said
GOLD STANDARD.

Hilary stood in the doorway and shouted, "That was
assault."

Jack said, "There's a railway station near here."

They climbed a grassy bank and ran beside a long
line of garden fences. A bend in a residential road was
fringed by cedar trees that overlooked the station.

They walked through the arched entrance.

The ticket office was closed.

A sign said LONDON TRAINS THIS WAY. They
jumped over a metal ticket barrier and ran through a glazed
underpass to the opposite platform. A yellow-and-white
train was arriving.

The carriage doors opened.

It was warm inside. The seats had high backs and
pointed towards the middle of the carriage.

Jack and Amy sat on either side of a white table.

The train pulled away.

Hilary ran up and banged on the window.

He shouted, "That was assault back there."

The train picked up speed. Meadows and hedges
flew past.

Amy said, "When do we get to the Peace Wall?"

"Only the enemy call it that. I don't think there is
one here."

Amy found a wedge-shaped plastic box on the seat
next to her. It had half a sandwich in it.

She looked at the packaging and said, "Roast
chicken salad."

"I thought you said you couldn't read."

"You have it. I'm not hungry."

She handed it to Jack. He took a bite of sandwich
and smiled.

"We really made it," he said.

"The Mouth was horrible."

Amy put her face in her hands and wept. Jack leant forward and touched her shoulder. She shrugged him off and rested her cheek on the window glass.

They went into a tunnel. Jack looked at his reflection. His khaki uniform had turned a light purple around the seams.

He said, "My face is different. I think my chin is a bit shorter."

"We have to find your grandfather."

"We could just disappear."

"What about the Resistance?"

Jack shrugged.

The train pulled in at a station and a recorded voice said, "This train is bound for Charing Cross."

A connecting door with the next carriage opened. A man in a dark uniform walked in. He wore a luminous green vest with RAILWAY ENFORCEMENT OFFICER written on it.

The man stopped beside their table and said, "Tickets please."

There was a long silence.

He said, "Can I see your tickets please?"

The connecting door opened again.

A muscular man walked in. He had blonde hair.

The guard said, "Do either of you have a ticket?"

The man tapped the guard's shoulder and said, "These two are with me. What do they owe you?"

Jack said, "I've never met this man before."

The man smiled. Sweat trickled down his chin.

He pulled a red banknote from a gold clasp and said, "I'm happy to pay for the tickets and any penalty fares or whatnot."

The guard said, "Who are you?"

"My name is Pierre Wilson. I work for a security company. These two young people are runaways—I've been hired to get them home to their parents."

Wilson took a card from the bottom of the clasp and handed it to the guard, who read it and scratched the back of his neck.

He said, "Do you accept this man's offer to pay?"

"Of course we accept," Amy said.

Jack turned to her and said, "What? No."

The guard said, "I'm going to contact the Transport Police in Charing. They can sort this out."

Amy said, "This man is who he says he is. We'd like him to pay."

The guard looked at Wilson.

"All right. May I see your ticket, sir?"

Wilson said, "Don't have one. I was in a bit of a rush. Look, no need to cart us all off in leg irons. Three tickets to London."

The guard tapped the screen of his handheld device. Tickets printed out of the back.

Wilson waited until the guard left the carriage and sat beside Jack.

The girders of a bridge flew past.

He said, "There are some people who want to have a word with you. Do as you are told and you won't get hurt."

The train crossed the Thames.

Amy pulled out a German Walther P38 9mm pistol from her waistband.

Wilson stared at the gun.

Amy said, "Search him."

Jack checked the man's pockets. There was the clasp of banknotes, a mobile phone and a small circular case that Jack unbuttoned. A pair of steel handcuffs fell onto the table.

Wilson said, "My firm knows where I am. If anything happens to me you are both dead."

Amy slid out from behind the table.

"Move," she said.

Jack pushed the security man off the seat.

She shoved the gun into Wilson's back.

They walked down the carriage and stopped by a door marked WC.

Amy said, "Open it."

She pointed to a porcelain lavatory bowl. There was a metal grab rail beside it.

Jack handcuffed Wilson to the bar.

Amy tucked the gun into the back of her trousers.

Jack slid the door shut.

The train pulled into the station.

Jack said, "There could be people waiting for us out there."

"Come on."

They walked down the platform to a steel barrier. A woman in front of them fed her ticket into a slot and a little gate sprang open.

Chapter Nine
The Catastrophe

Jack looked at the trim stone and brick station and said, "I can't believe how clean everything is."

Rows of globular lights hung from a vaulted ceiling.

Men and women stared up at boards showing train times.

Jack said, "Look at the glass tiles in the roof. Not a single pane broken."

Amy vomited greenish-purple fluid onto the tiled station floor. It spread into a translucent puddle.

She grabbed his arm and said, "We need to make contact with your grandfather."

They walked underneath a brick archway and came out on a cobbled forecourt. There were half a dozen black cars with TAXI signs on them.

They crossed a busy road and walked to a square where a towering column was guarded by bronze lions.

There was a church on one side. It had a tall spire. A man wearing a white leather coat sat at the bottom of the steps.

He said, "I don't suppose either of you two young people have any spare change?"

The man had pale hair and large, dark eyebrows.

He stared at them and said, "You look as though you've been on the streets for a bit, no offence. You looking for the night centre? You could get some food and a hot shower. They have clothes as well, no offence meant."

Amy said, "All right."

They followed him around the side of the church to the doorway of a nearby house.

He pushed the door open and said, "Best of British luck."

There was a corridor beside a room with chairs and sofas where half a dozen people sat and talked to each other.

A young man with oversized glasses and red-rimmed eyes said, "Hi there, I'm Rob."

Jack said, "I'm David, this is Ann."

Rob said, "Would you mind if I asked how old you guys are? It's just that if you are under sixteen I could get in touch with your local social Champions.

Amy said, "We're not. I was told you had clothes."

Rob said, "We have washing facilities too."

They followed Rob down a set of steps into a brick cellar.

He unlocked a metal wardrobe and said, "Help yourself. There are male and female bathrooms with soap and towels."

The water was hot.

Amy waited for him outside the door. She was wearing a red coat. Her face looked chalk-white without the layer of grime.

Jack's coat was yellow.

They walked up the stairs.

Amy coughed and spat green and purple phlegm on a step.

She said, "We're not staying here."

Rob was reading a newspaper.

He looked up and said, "Hi."

Amy said, "I need to get in touch with someone. I don't have their number."

Rob took out his mobile telephone and scratched his cheek.

He said "What is the name?"

"David Cunningham."

Rob said, "Do you know something specific about him?"

Jack thought for a moment and said, "He was a physics professor."

Rob said, "Here we go. University of Kent, retired. Wife Dr Ann Soper?"

Jack said, "That's him."

Rob wrote on a piece of paper.

He took it and said, "Thanks, come on Amy."

They went back into the cold night.

A man got out of a red van and walked towards them. He had a familiar muscular frame.

Wilson pointed an automatic pistol at them and said, "Give me the gun, now."

He made a beckoning gesture with his left hand.

Amy did nothing.

Wilson bought the grip of his automatic down on the bridge of her nose, grabbing the girl's hair as she fell.

Wilson pulled the pistol from her waistband as he slashed Jack's face with the barrel of his gun.

Jack lay on the road for a few seconds. Wilson buckled Amy into the passenger seat of the van. Her nose was bleeding.

Wilson pointed the gun at Jack and said, "Get in or I will kill you."

The security man climbed over them onto the driver's seat, turning the ignition and accelerating.

"Don't get any ideas," he said.

Jack leant across Amy and jammed his fist into Wilson's face. The van swerved into the pavement and hit a lamp post.

Jack opened the passenger door and fumbled with Amy's seat-belt.

The security man reversed the vehicle. Jack fell onto the road.

The red van raced off up the bus lane.

An electric lamppost lit up a flurry of snow.

A sign on a wall said, MEDE COLLEGE, LONDON. STRAND CAMPUS.

Wilson's pistol lay on the pavement. Snowflakes melted on the scuffed metal.

Jack picked it up.

An elderly black woman ran towards him.

She said, "Are you all right?"

Jack took Rob's piece of paper from his pocket and said, "I need to get to somewhere called Wanstead."

"Your mouth is bleeding."

"Do you know where it is?"

"Not sure. I think it's North London. On the border with Essex, maybe. You can get anywhere with a night bus from Trafalgar Square."

"Thank you."

He walked back to the square. Then he checked the routes displayed on the concrete posts of the glass bus stops.

He paid his fare with a banknote from Wilson's clasp and climbed up to the top deck.

Drunken passengers talked loudly to each other.

People got off at each stop until eventually he was alone.

Then the driver shouted, "This is the end of the line."

On the high street two young women walked past the ELEGANCE DRY CLEANER.

The bus drove off.

Jack wandered through a labyrinth of suburban villas and Victorian houses until he found Cunningham's road. He couldn't see anyone lying in wait for him.

He walked up to the house and rang the bell.

A voice from behind the door said, "Yes?"

Jack said, "Professor Cunningham?"

"Yes?"

"I need to speak to you."

"Who are you?"

"It's complicated. I'm your grandson."

"I have three grandchildren and they are all female," Cunningham said.

A woman's voice said, "David, who is it?"

Jack said, "I came through the Mouth. I need your help."

The professor unhooked the security chain.

Jack followed him into a cluttered living room.

Ann Soper stared at him. She had close-cropped white hair.

"My name is Jack. I need to know where Eustace Champion went before he took over the country—in the world I'm from."

The Cunninghams exchanged glances.

Ann said, "The Mouth project was mothballed here in the late nineteen forties. We have had no contact with anyone since then."

"Then I've come all this way for nothing," Jack said.

The professor touched his shoulder and said, "You've obviously been through a lot. By the looks of it any grandfather would be proud of you."

There was a tapping sound.

The professor went into the dining room and drew the curtains. Amy stood outside.

Jack said, "She's a friend. She came over with me."

Cunningham unlocked the back door and Amy walked in.

She said, "Are you David Cunningham?"

He said, "Yes."

Amy pulled the Walther out of her waistband and held it beneath the man's chin.

"This is for treason," she said.

The old weapon fired.

Chapter Ten
The Forest

Jack took Wilson's automatic out of his pocket and searched for the safety catch.

"Please. Wait," he said.

Amy turned her gun on the old woman.

Jack shot her in the chest. Amy crumpled forwards onto the floor.

Ann Cunningham knelt beside her dead husband.

Jack turned Amy over. Her eyes were open. Her pale face was speckled with the old man's blood and brains.

"You idiot, Amy."

"The Secret Intelligence Service waited forty years for someone to turn up with the missing Mouth."

"So all that stuff about your parents was a lie?"

"They are patriots. They sent me for re-education. I was assigned to watch the Mouth."

A patch of blood was expanding from the middle of her chest across her jumper. Jack took her hand and pressed on the wound.

He said, "These people are innocent."

"They are terrorists. You being here is proof of that."

A gun fired outside and a back window shattered.

Jack saw a shadow through the French windows and shot at it. He caught a glimpse of Wilson's surprised face before he disappeared into the darkness.

Ann Cunningham lay face-down on the floor.

Jack looked through the open door.

Wilson was spread-eagled on a flowerbed. There was a bullet hole in his left eye.

Jack went into the garden.

A voice behind him said, "That was a good shot."

Ann stood in the doorway, rubbing her forehead.

Jack showed her his baby index finger and said, "It was blown off by a mine and grew back in the Mouth. It has a mind of its own."

Ann said, "We didn't know who you were, Jack. We didn't tell you the truth about what we knew."

"I'm so sorry about David."

He looked through the broken window at Amy. Her eyes were closed.

"I should have known she was working for them."

Ann said, "I have made a resolution. I am going to stop Eustace Champion, or die trying. It's something we should have done a long time ago."

The faint wail of a police siren sounded in the distance.

Jack said, "I saw some woods coming here. Maybe I could hide."

"It's called the Epping Forest. Wait."

A few seconds later Ann came out with a white plastic bag.

She said, "A few things. A torch as well."

"Thank you."

The garden gate was open. He ran into a square of broken-up tarmac between two rows of dilapidated garages.

The area was bordered at one end by a wooden fence.

He swung over the top and landed on a privet hedge. His new yellow coat caught and he dangled in the air for a second before falling to the ground.

There was a winding street with houses on either side.

He crossed a busy road and ran into a field of long grass.

An ambulance drove past.

A sign said WANSTEAD FLATS.

Eddies of new snow twirled in the gusting wind.

He ran along the bank of a lake. Lampposts lining the road cast a pale glow on the surface of the water.

Dark clouds rolled over the stars. Snow spilled out of the sky.

The woodland became an ever-widening territory.

Soon he was in the deep forest walking amongst the stubby trunks of ancient pollarded trees.

He took the torch from the bag and switched it on.

Snow was falling through the gaps in the forest canopy.

There was a fallen beech tree.

He collected branches and lay half of them beside the tree. He weaved vines between the others to make a wall which he leant against the trunk.

Jack crouched for a minute and listened to the forest. Then he climbed inside.

Ann had packed a carton of pineapple juice and some sliced ham. Jack took a while working out how to open the juice. He wrapped himself in the rug.

A dog barked. Sunlight shone through the snow-filled cracks of the makeshift hide.

He heard a girl's voice.

A boot kicked a hole in the side of the shelter.

A man's voice said, "Anybody in there?"

A pair of gloved hands ripped out the wall of branches.

A square-jawed face looked down on him.

The man said, "Are you all right?"

Behind him, a dark haired woman held the reins of a plastic sled. A young boy and girl sat on it.

The man turned to them and said, "You go on ahead. I won't be long."

The woman hesitated for a second and said, "Okay."

She dragged the sled behind her.

The man said, "My name is Pye Oliver."

Jack stood up.

"I'm all right. Leave me alone."

"I work near here. For the council. I could try and find you somewhere to sleep tonight."

"I'm fine."

The man took off one of his gloves and searched in a trouser pocket.

He said, "There's a cafe by the road where you can get a cup of tea and breakfast. It looks like a log cabin."

He held out some coins.

Jack shook his head.

The man put the money back into his pocket.

"Promise me you won't sleep out here tonight. Even Robin Hood and his merry men couldn't survive winter in the forest. They had to hide out in Nottingham."

The square-jawed man turned and carried on up the path.

The log cabin cafe was at the edge of the forest.

Jack read a menu on the kiosk window and said, "Bacon sandwich please. And tea."

The woman behind the counter wore a white apron. She looked at his torn jacket and then up at his face.

"Rough night?"

"Yes."

Jack paid her from the clasp of the man he had killed.

He sat at a plastic table underneath the front awning.

Cars drove past along a snow-covered road.

Two chestnut-coloured horses rode into the car park behind the log cabin. The riders wore luminous jackets that said METROPOLITAN POLICE.

A female officer walked over to the kiosk and said, "Two teas, please."

She looked at Jack. The gaze lasted a moment too long.

She walked back to the car park and said something to her colleague. He pressed a radio on his shoulder and talked into it.

The woman officer returned to the kiosk and stood over Jack's table.

She said, "Excuse me sir. Would you mind if I asked you a few questions?"

Jack stood up and said, "Sorry, no, I don't have time."

He walked past her into the car park.

She followed him and said, "Someone answering to your description was involved in an incident in Wanstead yesterday. I would like to talk to you."

Jack said, "I don't mind at all, I need to take a quick leak, though."

"Are you aware you have blood on your clothing?"

"I can explain that."

He walked over to the horses.

The policewoman said, "Sir, where are you going?"

The other officer said, "She's talking to you."

Jack put his foot in the stirrup of the nearest horse and swung himself into the saddle.

The two officers ran towards him. The policeman grabbed his ankle.

Jack kicked the man's hand away and rode into the forest.

The animal was frightened and tried to knock him off by galloping beneath low branches. He clung to the horse's neck while the foliage whipped over him.

Then they raced up a footpath. Trees whirred past.

Jack saw a clearing ahead. The path narrowed and sloped downwards. The ground became rocky.

Jack said, "Steady, girl."

The animal stopped in front of a jutting boulder. Jack flew over the horse's shoulders and crashed into thick snow.

He was at the foot of a steep hill. Pye Oliver's wife and children shot past him on a plastic sled.

Jack ran up the slope into a line of dense woodland a police horse could not follow and buried his yellow coat in the snow.

Then he walked out of the forest into the cold backwaters of suburbia.

Chapter Eleven
The Two Books

*J*ack kept his head down and walked along pavements heaped with dirty snow. He passed a petrol station and turned up a hill.

There was a CONSERVATIVE CLUB and a mustard-coloured church.

He came to a seemingly never-ending street market whose stalls sold fruit, vegetables, flowers and clothes.

He browsed through a rack of coats, held up a black anorak and said, "How much?"

A man sitting on a plastic chair got up and said, "Thirty quid."

Jack paid him with notes from Wilson's money clasp.

He estimated the market was a mile long and walked up and down until the sun was low and the sellers were packing up their stalls.

He saw a policeman walking along the pavement and ducked into NEVILLE'S CARIBBEAN TAKEAWAY.

A copy of the WALTHAMSTOW GUARDIAN lay on a white counter. A headline on the front page said, "TWO DEAD IN WANSTEAD GUN BATTLE." There was a sketch of his face.

The owner of the restaurant said, "What can I get you, mate?"

Jack looked up at the photographs of food above the counter and said, "Jerk chicken."

The food came in a plastic box.

"Is there a telephone around here?"

"There's one in the square. No one uses it though. Even my nine-year-old has a mobile phone now."

The snow on the pavement was broken up by a line of wet salt.

The public telephone stood on a rectangle of pavement. He took out Rob's piece of paper, dropped some coins in the slot and punched the numbers.

A female voice said, "Hello."

Jack said, "Ann. It's me."

There was a pause.

"Hello Pamela. So thoughtful of you to call."

"Are the police there?"

"My daughter is here and there are two police officers."

"Right."

"I'll call you tomorrow, dear."

"Do they think I killed the man in the garden?"

"Yes. Goodbye."

Jack walked through the snow until he found a derelict house beside a railway bridge.

The windows were covered with metal security screens.

A sign on the front door said, DANGER UNSAFE TO OCCUPY.

He pushed the letter box open and looked through. Magazines and newspapers were heaped up against the door.

The garden was full of snow-topped weeds and bushes.

The security screen on one of the upstairs windows had been torn off. He pushed a plastic bin against the wall and climbed through the hole.

There was a ceramic bath behind a half demolished wall. A stained carpet was littered with hypodermic needles.

When his eyes adjusted to the dark, he saw an unzipped sleeping bag beside some cardboard boxes. He flattened them out and used them to line the bag. Then he pulled Ann's rug over him.

In the morning, Jack climbed out of the upstairs window, hung from the sill and dropped into the snow.

He ate breakfast in a café. Then he tried the telephone.

He said, "Ann?"

"Hello Pamela."

"Are they still there?"

"They said they would be leaving in a few hours."

"Okay."

"Thank you dear, goodbye then."

He made his way over to Ann's house when it started to get dark.

There were no Police cars in the street.

The garden gate was sealed with yellow POLICE LINE DO NOT CROSS tape. He ducked underneath it.

The back window had been replaced with a plywood screen.

He knocked on the French windows. Ann came out of the kitchen and opened a door.

She said, "David and I didn't tell you the truth. We weren't sure who you were."

The old woman pulled up a loose floorboard beneath the dining room table and took out two large, thin books.

She laid them on the table and opened each at the same page.

There were long columns of handwritten numbers on yellowing paper.

Ann said, "Each line of numbers shows the co-ordinates of a world that was visited by the first volunteers. Now, the book on the left was compiled over here, the other where you are from. All of the numbers in the books are completely identical to each other save for a single digit on a single line on a single page."

She pointed to the top line in the left-hand volume. It read, "[a81/05/71] [68/9016]." The right said, "[a81/05/71] [68/9017]."

Ann said, "The co-ordinates in my universe end with six. Yours with seven. One number decided the fate of your world and of mine. The seven is where your King Eustace went and got lucky. The six meant the narcissistic buffoon Eustace Champion remained a mediocre academic over here."

Jack said, "So these co-ordinates will take us to where King Eustace went?"

"Yes. But first we will have travel to your world—the seven only works over there."

"How do you know?"

"We tried it when Singh sent the book over from your world—just before the project was shut down over here. It didn't work. All the worlds are a little different. The Mouths are a little different. There is more than one version of the entity who sent the Mouth. Maybe infinite versions. The whole thing is quite complex, even for a physicist."

Ann ripped a page from the book and handed it to him.

She said, "I have memorised the co-ordinates. I suggest you do the same."

Boots crunched over snow outside.

A stocky man with a wispy beard stood on the lawn. He pointed a pistol-grip shotgun at them. The ugly weapon had a line of cartridges along the side.

They ducked.

The bullet shattered the door, showering them with glass.

There were more footsteps outside. Jack stood up and fired Wilson's automatic through the plywood screen.

He waited a few seconds and looked through the door. The man with the shotgun lay face down on the lawn.

"Another good shot," Ann said.

Jack searched the man's pockets. There was a set of car keys. A business card said, DAMIANO, AREA MANAGER, GOLD STANDARD SECURITY.

Ann said, "We need to be gone before the police arrive. You're already wanted for murder."

"Where to?"

"To Mede College. Eustace Champion still teaches there. That's where the Mouth is."

"I'll bet there's a red van near here."

The man in the garden was still breathing.

Jack picked up the shotgun. It had a canvas strap.

He swung the weapon over his shoulder and said, "Don't come after us."

They found the van in one of the garages. Ann drove them through the back streets.

Jack checked his guns as they circled a snowy roundabout.

Two police cars with blue flashing lights passed them.

They parked in a dark underpass that lay beneath the concrete facade of Mede College.

A gravel lane ended in a set of featureless three-storey buildings.

The front door had a triangular yellow sticker saying PREMISES PROTECTED BY GOLD STANDARD SECURITY.

Jack pointed to the first floor and said "There's a window open up there. I'll see if I can get in."

He shinned up a drainpipe and squeezed through a little window into a tiled lavatory.

There was a central stairwell. Jack ran down the steps to the front door.

Ann navigated them to a corridor at the back of the building.

Light spilled from a crack beneath a door.

Jack gave Wilson's gun to Ann.

She turned the handle. The door opened into a long room.

A conveyor belt led to a pedestal with a purple bowl on it.

A wizened man in a grey jacket was watching a younger man in red overalls load boxes.

Most of the containers were marked COMPUTERS. The younger man loaded a wicker hamper from FORTNUM AND MASON onto the belt.

The old man turned towards them.

Jack said, "Eustace Champion. I've seen that face on a few posters."

Champion said, "These are the people we were warned about, Duncan."

Duncan had dark hair and a red face. He put his hand in his pocket.

Jack pointed the shotgun at him and said, "Throw it over here."

Duncan took out a small revolver and dropped it on the floor.

"Now go away."

The man ran out of the door.

Ann pointed the automatic at Champion and said, "Hello, Eustace."

Champion said, "Ann. It has been a very long time."

"You murdered David."

"I had nothing at all to do with that. The girl exceeded her orders. I am very low down the pecking order, I assure you. His Majesty doesn't let me travel through the device. He gets very angry. He punishes me. I'm as much of a victim of him as you are."

There was a black DELL computer on a desk beside the Mouth. Ann sat down and typed a few keys.

She said, "The password."

Champion hesitated.

"*Vae victis*," he said.

Ann said, "Woe to the conquered. How apt."

Jack said, "Can you get it to work?"

"I designed the program this is based on," she said.

"We need an animal."

Ann held her arm out and fired Wilson's pistol. Champion clutched his neck and fell sideways.

"Here we go, decrypting the counterpart co-ordinates," Ann said.

The bowl turned a few degrees clockwise.

Jack propped the old man against the desk and rested his hand on the smooth purple surface.

"It's an altar. It demands sacrifice," Ann said.

The machine made a humming noise. Champion's fingers twisted and broke. The sleeve of his jacket went crimson. His arm detached and turned inside out. The old man fell onto the floor.

An arched rope of blood-flecked pink flesh rose above the basin. A blurred conveyor belt appeared on the other side of the membrane.

Jack said, "I don't want to go."

"What about your family? Or the millions King Eustace murdered?"

"It won't bring them back."

The old woman climbed onto the conveyor belt and waved her pistol in the air.

She said, "Tally ho!"

Jack hesitated for a heartbeat and followed her.

Part III: Vae Victis

Chapter Twelve
Audley Green

He knew what to expect this time. But that just made it worse. The seasons of agony ebbed and flowed. The memories are there but they are ugly and loveless. The Mouth was killing him again. Chewing him up. And then death—and then—

Jack fell onto Ann's back.

The conveyor belt was moving here.

The arch of flesh collapsed behind them.

An alarm bell was ringing.

Jack said, "Ann?"

The old woman was motionless. He turned her over. She had gone a light shade of purple. Her skin was cold. There was no pulse.

The conveyor belt ended and they fell onto the floor.

Jack looked at his hand. The trigger finger had completely grown back.

The room was as long and anonymous as the other one, except this one had three windows overlooking a dark cobbled square.

A door burst open and a man wearing an outsized peaked cap and olive-green uniform walked in. He had blue eyes and a cleft chin. There were purple epaulettes with gold tassels on his shoulders.

He said, "Curfew breaker!"

Jack pulled at the canvas strap of his shotgun. The material had fused with the skin on his shoulder.

The soldier unclipped a truncheon from his belt and hit Jack's neck. The weapon rained down on him until things went black.

He was dragged down a corridor.

A brown Wolseley motorcar pulled up in the dark courtyard.

He saw campus buildings through the window.

The car drove beside the Thames. The lamp posts on the riverbank were not working but the river reflected rippling moonlight onto the bare branches of London plane trees.

The Wolseley crossed Westminster Bridge. The gothic buildings Jack remembered from pictures in old books had been replaced by a giant triangular structure that filled the skyline.

Jack fought to stay conscious. He dreamt he was trying to swim but his hands had no fingers.

He opened his eyes and looked up at ceiling tiles. They were covered in grime.

His hands and feet were manacled to the corners of a cast-iron bed.

He coughed. A stabbing pain in his ribs made him cry out.

The door opened and a nurse walked in. She had purple hair.

She unhooked an empty intravenous bag from a metal pole beside his bed.

Jack said, "Where am I?"

The nurse took a gag from a hook on the wall and fixed it in his mouth.

She hung a new bag of clear liquid on the pole.

Jack closed his eyes.

He woke to find a white-haired soldier at the end of his bed.

"Do you know who I am?"

"Audley-Green. The mass murderer."

The old man made a snorting, delighted laugh as he walked around the bed.

"I've heard you murdered one of our brave agents. She's alive, incidentally. Who sent you back here to kill King Eustace? Answer and I might let you live."

"You are a lunatic."

General Audley-Green threw the folder of notes against the wall. Paper fluttered in the air.

He said, "You beastly fellow! I know about the Cunninghams. But who is behind them?"

The old man examined the metal tray on Jack's bedside table and said, "I don't do much clinical work nowadays. I miss it."

The General fixed a needle onto a hypodermic syringe and said, "I'm sending you on a little trip to the countryside for a spot of graded environmental exercise. A team of first-class physicians will get the truth out of you."

Audley Green filled the syringe from a glass vial and stuck the needle in the boy's arm.

"Life expectancy is not good down there, so I would co-operate if I were you."

Jack woke up sitting on a bench in the back of a moving lorry. He wore ankle chains that were threaded through a ring in the floor. His bare feet were numb with cold.

The canvas compartment cover rustled in the wind.

A boy soldier sat on the opposite bench. He wore the dark blue uniform of the Royal Political Protection Agency.

A black bull mastiff lay on the floor.

The boy soldier said, "My name is Corporal Ivory. If I hear a peep out of you, I will kill you. Then I will feed you to my dog. Working in a death camp has given him a taste for human flesh."

Jack closed his eyes. The vehicle bounced along a dirt road. When he woke, the Bedford had stopped.

Ivory unlocked Jack's chains and shoved him out of the vehicle.

Wild flowers grew amongst acres of chalk rubble.

There was a giant electrified fence held up by tall concrete pillars. A watch tower had a big gate in its middle.

A disused railway line terminated in front of the camp.

Ivory shoved Jack through a small pedestrian gate beside the tower.

A sign said, CHISLET NEURO-PSYCHOSOCIAL REHABILITATION CENTRE. A CENTRE OF EXCELLENCE.

A group of prisoners marched across a muddy courtyard. Their dirty faces were sunken and expressionless. A spoon and tin mug hung around each neck.

Ivory pushed him through the doorway of a single-storey concrete building.

The room smelt of pipe smoke. Files and ledgers were piled up against each wall. A man sat behind a plastic desk. He was mostly bald and scraped his remaining hair over the top of his head.

Ivory said, "Reporting with prisoner, Mr Nixon."

The man held out a hand. Corporal Ivory placed an envelope in it.

Mr Nixon opened it and said, "Your notes say you are from the Curfew so I'll call you Curfew Rat."

Jack said, "I need some shoes."

Nixon put his coat on and said, "We don't encourage escape. Let's get you tucked up for the night, shall we?"

The guard led him along a muddy path.

There were identical corrugated-iron shelters on either side. Each was made of a single sheet of metal that had been bent into a semicircle. Sandbags were stacked at either end.

Nixon stopped beside a sign that said, HUT 91, UNEXPLAINED MEDICAL SYMPTOMS.

He said, "Here we are."

Prisoners sat on filthy blankets that lined each side of the shelter. There was frost on the muddy floor.

Nixon said, "Find yourself a space. We had two deaths today so there should be plenty of room."

Jack found some unoccupied bedding and sat on it. No one spoke. Rain drummed on 'the roof. The prisoners lay down.

Five minutes later the light went off.

Chapter Thirteen
Curfew Rat

The prisoners on either side of him turned over and hunched up onto their knees and elbows.

Jack whispered, "What's happening?"

A voice nearby whispered, "Saves body heat."

Another voice said, "Quiet. The screws will hear."

They were woken a few hours later by a voice that came from a tannoy outside the hut.

It said, "An opportunity is now available for all prisoners to voice their respect for our wise and glorious leader Professor King Eustace the first."

The prisoners filed out of the hut.

A thick-set man wearing a nurse's top read the numbers on their overalls.

He held out a hand and stopped Jack.

"Curfew Rat. You have an appointment this morning. Report to the Total Modification Building."

Jack followed the crowd into a rubble courtyard.

There were hundreds of prisoners, their shrunken bodies wrapped in filthy rags. Dirty faces were webbed with scar tissue.

A young woman stood in front of an empty grinny. Her hands were manacled to the pole behind her. She had a gag in her mouth and was trying to say something.

The prisoners watched her in silence while the sun rose.

A voice came over the public address system.

It said, "Welcome Warden Orme."

Everybody clapped.

A thin man wearing a cashmere overcoat walked through the square to a table where he picked up a microphone. His dark eyes studied the crowd.

He took a piece of paper from his coat pocket and said, "Prisoner TF29472 witnessed an escape attempt last week and did not report it. This is the sign of an untreatable maladaptive behavioural pattern. The sentence is death. Long live the King."

Six riflemen from the Royal People's Army formed a line. A member of the squad placed a wooden box over the woman's head. It had a circular target painted on the front.

Prisoner TF29472 danced a small, defiant jig.

The firing squad leader said, "Ready your weapons. Aim at the enemy. Fire."

There was a ragged volley.

The young woman's head jerked back and the box fell off, revealing streaming gray hair. Her face was a mass of blood. She slid to her knees.

A voice came over the loudspeakers. It was a recording of King Eustace.

"You have seen how the beastly fellows who fail re-education end up. Live a decent English life without disease."

The squad put white gloves on. One of them looped barbed wire around the woman's neck.

The others hoisted her body up the grinny.

Violin music came over the camp speakers. The prisoners sang, swaying with the melody as the body was hoisted up the pole.

"We have nothing to envy,
With science on our side.
We have no sickness to fear,
With King Eustace as our guide."

The music stopped and the crowd dispersed.

Jack asked a bent-backed prisoner the way to Total Modification. She pointed to a brick building beyond the huts.

A thick-set man in reception said, "My name is Nurse Digory. Any trouble and you'll get a slap."

They walked up a white hallway to the TREATMENT SUITE 3.

The room had a tiled floor. There was a hosepipe in the corner.

Digory poured coal from a scuttle into a wide metal urn.

The nurse unbuttoned Jack's overalls, rolled them to his waist, manacled the boy's ankles and hung them over a hook. He pressed a red button on the wall. A chain hanging from the ceiling tightened until Jack was dangling upside down.

A man strode into the cell. He wore a pinstripe suit and smelled of aftershave.

"Good morning. I am Lord Amhurst, the senior consultant in charge of your care."

"Can you let me down, please? The blood is going to my head."

Amhurst lit a cigar and said, "I'll be honest with you. We can do this the easy way or the hard way. It's your responsibility."

"Why have you hung me upside down?"

"It's called environmental modification. Your surroundings are altered to change the way you think about yourself. So, let's start with your name."

"What about it?"

"What is it? Come now, even a captured soldier gives his name, rank and number."

"I'm not a soldier."

"Yet you were carrying a gun when they arrested you. Who was behind the plot to kill our beloved leader?"

"I don't know. I suspect General Audley-Green."

"I can't work with this. All right Nurse, let's begin the procedure."

Digory handcuffed Jack's wrists and shackled them to the boy's ankles so his belly faced the floor. His body became a painful arc.

The nurse shoved the burning coals underneath him and pressed a button on the wall.

As the chain extended and Jack was lowered Amhurst said, "People like you Curfew Rat are the reason we needed King Eustace. Your sense of victimhood is pathetic. You are the aggressor. We are your victims."

Jack's skin touched the coals and he cried out.

Amhurst said, "Live or die, your choice. Let's start with your name, shall we?"

The door swung open. Mr Nixon ran into the room with a piece of paper.

Amhurst read it.

"All right nurse, abandon the procedure."

Digory said, "Sir?"

"Move the coals you idiot."

The consultant puffed on his cigar and said, "In two days his Majesty will be coming here to personally conduct a ward round. In the meantime I'm going to prescribe a course of vigorous scientific graded exercise."

He wrote something in a notebook and walked out.

Nurse Digory returned with a trolley. He knelt down and ran a thumb over Jack's stomach.

Jack said, "I thought you brainwash boys didn't believe in medicine."

Digory took a tube from the trolley and squeezed a bulb of white ointment onto the palm of his hand. He rubbed the cream over the boy's belly.

A guard knocked on the door. The man had a lined face. There were broken veins on his nose.

He said, "Taking custody of Prisoner B153218 Curfew Rat."

Digory unhooked the chain.

Jack fell onto the tiles.

He followed the guard over the rubble square into a bomb-damaged expanse of broken masonry.

The man stopped beside a half-collapsed ABC CINEMA. He pointed to a tower on the horizon with a wheel above it.

Jack followed a group of prisoners between two hills of black spoil.

The sign at the entrance to the metal tower said, CHISLET MINE. GOLD STANDARD ENVIRONMENTAL AND EXERCISE THERAPY. DESIGNED BY HRH AT MEDE COLLEGE, LONDON.

The lift cage was suspended from the wheel above the tower.

He joined a large crowd of prisoners. Then he saw a familiar face. It was covered in coal dust but he recognized the scars. He stood on his toes to get a better look and their eyes met. It was Badger.

The cage refilled every few minutes. Each time the crowd moved forward a few feet. With every surge Jack pushed himself forward until he stood beside Badger.

They got into the cage together. The lift descended. Badger did not meet Jack's gaze as they went down into the darkness.

Faint electric light shone through the mesh floor as they emerged into a chamber hundreds of feet wide.

The cage bumped to a stop.

They joined a line of people queuing in front of a wooden desk.

A soldier wearing the olive green uniform of the Royal People's Army wrote numbers down in a thick ledger. He had a moustache. A wooden truncheon hung on the side of his chair.

"Name?"

Badger said, "Dudley Clements."

"Bay 27a."

Jack said, "Curfew Rat."

"Same bay. You're at the top so fill your tub quickly or you'll hold the others up."

They selected metal tools from a heap in the centre of the cavern and lit their lamps from a communal candle.

Badger walked into a service tunnel. He turned and hugged Jack.

Jack said, "I thought you were dead."

"So did I. One bullet grazed my eyebrow and the other bounced off my rib. A couple of brainwash boys saw me outside town. I woke up in this place."

Badger unbuttoned his boiler suit and pulled it open. There was a line of deep scar tissue across his ribs. His belly was covered with dog bites.

He said, "There's no medicine here. They leave you in a hut and either you get better or you snuff it. It's called enhanced recovery. I was lucky."

Jack said, "The ferrets got everyone back home."

"Sorry to hear that."

They walked into tunnel 27.

The coal seam crackled faintly from the weight above it.

A metal tub sat on a rail track.

Badger drove a metal wedge into the wall with a hammer. He prised out a long rectangle of coal. They jumped out of the way as it shattered on the floor, filling the air with soot.

They shovelled the pieces into a wheelbarrow. Then Badger upended the little vehicle's load into the tub.

He said, "Sod it. They're lining up behind us."

Jack looked back down the tunnel. He could see a few tiny figures standing beside their tubs.

"Let's move the tub then."

"It has to be full. They do spot checks."

A soldier ran towards them.

Badger dropped his axe and stood in front of the wall with his hands behind his head.

Something hard hit Jack's cheekbone. He fell against the coal seam and blacked out for a second. Hot blood trickled out of his nose.

The soldier said, "Lazy, lazy, lazy. Next time I'll bloody well brain the both of you."

They worked silently on the seam until the metal tub was full.

Badger crouched behind the vehicle and released the brake. They pushed the heavy load up a steep gradient.

The tunnel levelled out. Badger stopped to pull a lever. The tub swung to a left-hand track.

He said, "I want to get back to the Curfew. It wasn't much of a life but it was better than this."

"I found a burned-out Resistance Station. Then something happened you wouldn't believe unless you'd seen it yourself."

"What was it?"

"A device that opens a door into another world."

Badger laughed.

"Like Mars?"

"No. I went to a different England where the pogroms, the murders and the camps hadn't happened."

They pushed the tub into a cavernous chamber. Badger said, "Here we are."

A circular conveyor belt looped around the room before sloping steeply upwards to a far-off square of daylight.

Badger slotted the coal tub onto a tippler and turned the handle of a wheel. The vehicle rotated until the coal tumbled onto one of the recessed troughs that conveyed the load to the little square of sky.

As they pushed the empty tub out of the cavern Badger said, "Why did you come back here, if this other place was so good?"

"I met someone over there who thought she could change things. She's dead."

"We will we be too if we stay in this place for much longer."

"Yes."

Chapter Fourteen
Explosives

*B*adger hammered a metal wedge into the coal seam and said, "This place isn't about coal. It's about power. You agree with their stupid theories or they kill you."

Jack held his hands up to the lamp. There were white blisters on his palm and the insides of his fingers.

He said, "King Eustace is coming down from London. He's going to torture me to death."

Badger pulled the wedge out and said, "We can't have that now, can we? What say you and me get out of here?"

"I don't know if you've noticed but we're in a death camp with a bloody great electrified fence around it."

Badger scratched his chin and said, "Half a dozen tunnels have collapsed in the last week—there's not enough timbering to hold them up."

"So?"

"A feller told me that when one goes the screws don't even bother rescuing the prisoners. They just leave them to die."

Badger tapped the ceiling with his knuckles and said, "We could cause a collapse. Make it look like we've been crushed. The Royal Politicals won't search for dead prisoners."

He pulled up a trouser leg. There were three sausage-shaped wraps of greaseproof paper tied to his calf.

He said, "Nitroglycerine. For blasting. And fuse wire. They use explosives to make new tunnels. I did a couple of shifts."

"How long have they been there?"

"Few days."

"You could have blown yourself up."

Badger unwound the wire and handed the explosives to Jack.

Then he ran a finger along the tunnel roof.

"Perfect. It's carrying way too much weight. There's a nice bulge in the middle."

He drove the metal wedge into the ceiling and twisted it a few times. Then he pushed a charge into the hole, scooped debris from the floor and packed it around the explosive.

They moved up the tunnel. Badger made a second cavity and Jack pushed explosive into it. Jack set the last charge.

He said, "How far away do we have to be?"

Badger tied the individual wires to a long fuse.

"As much as possible."

Badger took the top from his lamp and held the burning wick up to the fuse.

They ran a hundred yards before the noise of three sharp, rapid blows filled the tunnel and a shock wave knocked them over. There was a rending sound and the walls shook. A wall of coal dust blew up the tunnel.

Badger coughed and said, "Come on."

They followed the rails into the big cavern.

The conveyor belt was moving.

Jack sat in a coal tray and said, "Any plan for when we get outside?"

Badger climbed into the shallow trough behind him. "We'll make something up."

They watched the little window of daylight grow in size until the radiance enveloped them.

Then they were outside in gusting, swirling rain.

Jack stuck his head over the side. The moving belt was high above the ground, held up by towering metal pillars.

There was a long line of open-backed Bedford lorries in the works yards ahead of them.

The guard tower was a shadow in a grey mist.

Badger said, "Hope nobody is looking up."

The belt inclined downwards. Beneath them, two guards sheltered under a tarpaulin lean-to before a party of prisoners who knelt in the mud with their hands behind their heads.

The conveyor trundled towards the lorries. The escapees lay back in their troughs.

The belt ended suddenly and Jack flew into the air. He saw his blackened feet against the sky.

Then he hit the floor of an open-topped container. Badger fell beside him.

The tailgate of the big metal box was hinged at the bottom. Chains hung on either side of it.

Badger pulled himself up and stuck his head over the top.

He swung down and said, "Too many people. A couple of screws. And soldiers."

A lump of coal bounced on the metal floor. They looked up.

A fountain of coal cascaded over the end of the conveyor belt into the Bedford. Clouds of black dust were thrown up in ever-thickening waves as the coal formed into an expanding heap. Jack grabbed a chain and climbed up until his head was flush with the top of the container.

The mound of coal took a few seconds to reach his feet. Then his legs were pushed up against his chest. Soon the coal engulfed him, squeezing the air from his body and entombing him in painful darkness.

He pushed his head out and sucked in air.

The lorry drove to the guard tower. He felt rain on his face. The huge electric gates swung outwards and they left the camp.

He got his arms free and pushed himself upwards. In a few seconds he had worked his way to the surface.

The Bedford sped along a muddy track.

The rain made the heaped coal slippery.

Jack crawled to the top of the mound and said, "Badger?"

The vehicle hit a pothole and he slid down to the other side of the container.

Badger's head emerged out of the dark rock.

He said, "Get me out of here."

Jack crooked his arms under the man's armpits and pulled. Badger man grunted and pushed.

The Bedford bounced a few times, sending them sliding across the coal to the front of the trailer. They sheltered from the rain behind the driver's cab.

"I'm staying on until it gets to London," Jack said, "I have things to do there."

"This lorry is delivering coal to a curfew garrison. We're going south. To the coast."

The wasteland gave way to green bushes and woodland.

The Bedford braked suddenly.

The door of the front cab opened.

The rain was falling hard now.

Jack said, "Go around the back and distract him."

The soldier held a waterproof cape over his head and ran over to the bushes lining the muddy road.

Jack climbed over the side and hung from the edge of the container for a second. He dropped onto the mud and rolled under the vehicle.

Badger landed noiselessly and disappeared into the trees.

The soldier unbuttoned his trousers.

Jack crawled to the driver's cab and opened the passenger door. A bayonet hung from the driver's seat, tangled up in some canvas webbing. He looked through the window and saw Badger emerge from the trees.

"Sorry mate, you're not allowed to piss here. It's against the rules."

The Curfew soldier threw his cape on the floor and held up a Lee Enfield rifle at Badger.

Jack unsheathed the long blade from its scabbard and ran around the front of the cab.

The soldier said, "Say goodnight Noddy."

Jack stuck the bayonet into the back of the man's neck. The soldier turned and tried to pull it out. The three of them stood for a second before the man crumpled onto the ground.

Jack said, "Sorry. I didn't reckon he would take his rifle with him."

Badger checked the man's pockets.

He brought out a bronze halfpenny and said, "Toss you for his boots. Heads or tails? "

Jack looked down. The man's blood was puddling in the muddy road.

He said, "You have them."

They searched the cab.

"Two pouches of ammo. And a water bottle," Badger said.

He took a gulp.

The hum of a diesel engine sounded in the distance.

Jack took an ammo pouch. Badger grabbed the rifle. They ran into the trees.

"We could take them," Badger said.

"There'll only be another one right behind him. We can't take on the whole British army."

Badger laughed.

"The last time I helped you I ended up in a re-education camp."

They ran through the trees together. In a few minutes, they were in open country.

Chapter Fifteen
The Old Hospital

A wide plain of marshland stretched out to the horizon. Chunks of concrete lay amongst tufts of long grass and pools of dark water. Scraps of fabric fluttered on the end of rusty metal rods.

Badger stopped running and put his hands on his knees.

He said, "Stop a second. I'm puffed out."

Jack sat on a block of concrete. There was a clump of hair sticking out from underneath it. He got up. The big stone fell sideways and rolled into a dark pool. A puffy white face floated up to the surface of the water. Bubbles rose up and gave off an ugly smell. The forehead was caved in on one side.

Badger said, "You found something?"

"People."

Badger kicked a lump of aggregate over. A rib cage stuck out of a duffle coat.

"From London, judging by the clothes," he said.

"The Medicine Man said smallpox was back. The King said it was an apocryphal sickness belief."

"That bloke has got a lot to answer for."

They ran over the marshland and climbed up a grassy ridge. A gust of wind blew them over.

Then they were looking out at an enormous wave-torn sea.

"I never thought I'd get to see this," Badger said.

They walked up to the edge of a chalk cliff and looked down at the beach.

Beneath them towering missiles, radar control equipment and antenna sat on a twelve-foot-wide never-ending strip of concrete that cut the beach in half and wound around the shoreline. All of the rockets pointed out to the sea.

They sat on the cliff edge.

Two seagulls hovered in the breeze.

Half a mile out to sea waves pounded a second continuous line of steel-skinned ballistic rockets.

Badger said, "The Great Patriotic Sea Wall. Built by slave labour like everything King Eustace makes."

A patch of ocean glittered where the clouds had parted.

Jack said, "I remember some of the rockets from the old Resistance spotting guides. The really tall, thin ones on the beach are Longbow Anti-Ship Incendiaries. They stopped the NATO expedition."

Jack looked down at a squat rocket on the beach below the cliff edge and said, "That thing below us is an Intercontinental Bulldog."

Jack threw a clod of earth at the missile's nose cone. The rivets holding the metal war machine together had rusted to a dark brown. The soil struck and scattered in the wind.

Badger took the soldier's boots off and handed them to his companion.

Jack said, "What about you?"

Badger held up a pair of sodden suede shoes and turned them upside down. Droplets of brown water scattered in the wind.

He said, "I don't think the previous owner would mind."

They walked over undulating cliffs. Later the headland sloped down to the beach.

They stood a hundred yards from a line of high-calibre machine guns with disc-shaped sensors mounted on their backs.

Jack said, "Anti-personnel sentries. Browning 50mm by the looks of it."

Badger picked up a pebble and lobbed it at one of the machine guns. It hit the weapon with a metallic tang.

The gun swivelled around and they flattened themselves on the stones.

Jack said, "That wasn't very clever."

The machine made a whirring sound and swung back.

More rain fell. They walked to the top of a grassy ridge.

Beneath them, a section of chalk cliff had fallen onto the beach, burying the line of war machines beneath it.

The tips of some rockets peaked out of the water, crimped out of shape by the rock fall and covered with barnacles.

Jack said, "Why didn't the brainwash boys mend this?"

"Maybe they don't know how to. There was always rumours he got help from somewhere in the early days. Could be whoever built it has gone."

Badger turned towards the land and pointed to a line of pine forest in the far distance.

He said, "I vote we make a shelter before it gets dark. Maybe brew a cup of pine needle tea."

A gust of rain blew across the marshes.

As they walked the outline of a massive domed building rose from behind the trees.

There was an abandoned road at the edge of the pines.

Jack tore weeds off a metal sign that said KINGS WOOD. A CENTRE OF ROBUST SCIENTIFIC EXCELLENCE.

The pot-holed tarmac track took them to a tall electric fence. Wildflowers were growing up the concrete posts. One support had fallen and pulled its metal wires to the ground. They crossed over it into the compound.

Ahead of them, there was a colossal brick building with a concrete dome. It stood in the middle of a rubble wasteland.

There was a thirty-foot high metal door. A sign said EVACUATION ORDER. THIS FACTORY IS UNDER PERMANENT CURFEW.

The door was mounted on casters. There was a pull bar.

"You feeling strong?" Badger said.

They heaved. There was a rending sound. A gap of a few inches opened up. A smell of rust and damp wafted out.

Jack and Badger squeezed through the opening.

A line of windows high up in the building cast the only light into the cavernous gloom.

Murals of smiling workers were painted around the wall.

Thousands of derelict machines encircled a giant statue of a young King Eustace. He wore workers overalls and had a pencil behind his ear.

Robotic machines with blades for arms sat in front of redundant assembly lines.

Their new shoes crunched on broken bulbs and metal coils.

A stubby aeroplane hung from a hydraulic grabbing arm. The grabber and the fuselage were brown with rust but the bulbous nose was made from a purple substance that had not aged.

Badger said, "Looks like one of the unmanned Mosquitoes from the start of the war. Bloody lethal things. No hiding from them, my Dad said. Well, doesn't look like there's anything to eat here."

They left the factory and walked up a path that led to a brick building. It had round turrets at each corner. Hundreds of windows reflected the late afternoon sun.

A flight of stone steps led up to a terrace of cracked paving stones. A sign said KINGS WOOD CHILDREN'S BEHAVIOURAL UNIT. THE GOLD STANDARD OF EXCELLENCE.

Badger said, "If it's a hospital there might be some tinned grub."

They looked into a giant plate glass window. There was a room with a long wooden counter. A sign on the wall said RECEPTION.

Badger threw a brick at the window. It bounced off. He pointed his rifle at the glass.

Jack said, "Someone could hear. There's probably a way in around the side."

They walked around the building and found a plywood door. Badger put his boot through it.

The room had a musty smell. Jack picked up a magazine from the floor. It said, THE COMET, A JOURNAL OF PSYCHOLOGICAL SCIENCE. APRIL 1981. H.M. KING EUSTACE DISPROVES NUMEROUS APOCRYPHAL SICKNESS BELIEFS IN CHILDREN, SAYS "THIS IS A WONDERFULLY PROVOCATIVE STUDY" AND "A THING OF BEAUTY".

They climbed a flight of steps. A sign above a doorway said SOMATIZATION REVERSAL. The room had neat rows of wooden cots on either side.

Badger said, "I wouldn't want to be a kid here."

"Nor me."

The stairs led to more wards and treatment rooms before finally terminating in front of a red door. There was gold lettering on it that said LORD VERE-WATSON. MD FRCPsych. PRIVATE.

Badger turned a brass handle. The door swung inwards.

There was a wood-panelled entrance hall. Two fur coats hung off a hat stand. Badger took one and handed the other to Jack.

A spacious living room was lined with bookshelves and brightly coloured oil paintings.

A gilt-edged portrait of a dark-haired man with a round face hung above a fireplace.

A pair of sliding white doors led into a dining room. Two dead bodies were slumped over a long table that was set for a dinner party.

A dark-haired man who resembled the painting above the fire had a pick axe in the back of his head. His face had dried into an almost translucent grey-green husk. Most of his blue woolen smoking jacket had been eaten by moths.

A younger man opposite him had been garrotted with a piano wire. It hung from a deep cut in his sinewy neck.

The room still had a faintly malign smell.

Badger checked the jacket pockets of the dead men and found a box of matches. He lit a candle in a silver candlestick.

A folding door led into a kitchen with a cooker and a yellow Formica table.

There was a green door in a side wall. A sign said, LARDER, PERSONS CAUGHT STEALING WILL BE SENT TO THE SECURE UNIT—LORD V.W.

Badger opened the door and held up the candle. Several rats ran out.

Packs of QUAKER OATS, FORCE TOASTED WHEAT FLAKES and SILVER SPOON SUGAR had been chewed open and eaten.

Badger took out a tin of BROWN WINDSOR VEGETABLE SOUP and shook it.

He said, "I think this one is all right."

Jack selected a can of SMEDLEY'S ENGLISH RED DESSERT PLUMS.

Badger said, "I told you we should come here."

He found a can opener in a drawer, drank a few gulps and passed it to Jack.

A hallway led to a big room. It had a double bed and a tall chest of drawers in the corner.

There was a glass door leading to a stone balcony. The setting sun cast a faint light over two rotting deckchairs.

Badger lay down on the bed. Jack tried the drawers in the chest. Most were full of expensive clothes that had been eaten by moths.

Then he found a piece of blue carbon paper under a pair of striped pyjamas.

Badger said, "Anything interesting?"

"Don't know."

"Read it out."

"My name is Mark Vere-Watson. I am one of the architects of the great re-education established when his Majesty King Eustace assumed power.

"We both believed that we could end the distinction between mind and body using psychological treatments to banish sickness and usher in a new golden age of health and happiness for mankind."

Badger said, "He sounds like a brainwash boy."

"I am one of the most respected physicians in the land and have served my country with great patriotism for many years. But within the last few days I have come into conflict with his Majesty King Eustace over my private life. For some years I have had a happy and fulfilled relationship with a companion who I love dearly. That person happens to be a man. On learning this His Majesty has told me I must undergo Hetero-Normative Behavioural Therapy."

"I do not need re-education. I above all people know that it is a sham. I realised many years ago Eustace is a fanatic. His triumph over disease was no such thing. Those patients who do not validate his theories are still being murdered or worked to death in the camps. I have watched so many die in agony. I only helped him because I wanted to stay alive."

"I am resolved to travel through an extraordinary device that I discovered by chance several years ago in the King's private office in Buckingham Palace."

"I bribed a technician and successfully travelled to another world - an England where I discovered having a partner of your choice is not a criminal act. We will travel there next week."

Jack stopped reading and said, "The Mouth. So. That's where I have to go. Buckingham Palace. I told you, Badger."

"I never doubted you. Now if you don't mind I think I'll have forty winks."

Jack lay beside him on the bed and closed his eyes.

The sound of war machines came through the glass door. Jack ran onto the stone balcony.

The factory was on fire. Light flickered in the high windows. The dome made a crackling sound and the top collapsed inwards. Orange fire shot up the dark sky.

Badger stood in the door and said: "They really don't like you."

Two Centurion tanks drove across the wasteland towards them.

A helicopter shone a searchlight on the hospital building.

They ran through Lord Vere-Watson's apartment and down the stairs into the reception room.

Light glinted on the heat suits of an advancing mobile fire unit.

They ducked behind the counter.

Jack said, "The door. You could make it. They're here for me."

"Not necessarily. Don't be so big-headed."

A Royal Political Protection agent wiped a patch of glass with his elbow.

He looked inside and said, "Right, fellas let's get this window down."

One of the ferrets adjusted the silver nozzle on his flamethrower. A long jet of liquid fire broke over the glass. The window blackened for a split second and shattered.

Gouts of flame roared over them.

Boots squeaked on the reception room floor. The agent leant over the counter and grabbed Jack. Badger worked the bolt on the Lee Enfield and shot. The man stood for a second. Blood dribbled from a bullet hole above his nose. It caked his moustache and dribbled down the side of his chin. He fell backwards.

Badger fired at the ferrets, who ducked.

The fugitives jumped over the counter and ran through the side door. An explosive river of flame roared out after them a few seconds later.

They held up the high-tension wires of the fence for each other. Then the escapees made for the marshland beyond the pine trees.

Chapter Sixteen
Olly

Two figures ran across the cliffs. The endless line of rockets on the beach pointed out at the dark sea.

Badger stopped by a burned-out village, put up his hand and said, "Let's rest a minute."

Jack pulled a tin of plums from the pocket of his fur coat and said, "Can I borrow the bayonet?"

Badger twisted the blade off the rifle. Jack cut the top off the can. The plums were still sweet.

Further up the coast another section of the cliff had collapsed into the sea, burying the inner line of war machines completely.

The noise of a flying machine sounded in the air. A searchlight swept over them.

It lit up two towers.

A flint wall between them had a bricked-in doorway.

Waves lapped at one side.

The helicopter flew over them.

They ran around the side of the ruin. There was a warren of ragged stone walls behind the towers. Most were only a few feet high.

"The beach defences are all underwater and out of use here. I can swim out to sea and flank them. Keep them talking."

"All right."

Badger handed the rifle over and said, "Start counting to a hundred."

He put the bayonet between his teeth and dived into the water.

Jack crouched down behind one of the ancient stone barriers and stared through a crack. Three people ran over the grassy promontory ahead of him. One wore the blue one-piece of the Royal Political Aviation Service. The other two wore silver heat suits.

The men disappeared behind an apron of broken stones.

An amplified voice said, "Good morning, gentlemen. We've had quite a time finding you. My compliments. I want this to be civil. My name is Oliver, my friends call me Olly."

Jack saw the tops of two silver helmets.

He said, "So why did you bring ferrets with you?"

Olly said, "Look mate, I just fly helicopters. I'm not one of those political blokes. You and your friend come out slowly with your hands behind your heads, eh?"

A flint pebble fell from a wall. The pilot light on a flamethrower nozzle glowed blue and hissed.

Olly said, "King Eustace personally ordered this mission. His Majesty will give us merry hell if we bring you back dead."

"In that case, I have some demands."

"To be honest with you mate that's probably pushing your luck a bit."

Jack put the Lee Enfield rifle to his shoulder and stood up.

"One hundred," he said, and fired.

The pilot opened his mouth. He had a loudhailer in one hand and a pistol in the other. A red mark appeared on his chest.

Then there were two shots from a high powered rifle.

A fuel tank exploded with a massive boom, flooding the grassland with liquid fire and knocking him onto his back. Black smoke engulfed everything.

A voice far away said, "Jack? You all right?"

Badger's face appeared through the smoke. He was carrying a black rifle with a telescopic sight.

He pulled Jack to his feet and said, "They had a bloke trying to flank us. The water was freezing. My teeth were chattering so hard I thought he would hear me coming up behind him."

The man who had called himself Olly lay on a patch of blackened grass. His steaming torso gave off a scent of roast pork and diesel.

Jack said, "We were lucky."

"Luck had nothing to do with it. The Royal Curfews are streaks of piss. They're used to picking on cave men."

The body of a ferret hung over a wall. The back of his helmet had a hole in it.

There was no sign of the man whose fuel tank had exploded.

The sun rose as they walked behind the beach. Surf rattled over the shingle.

Trees appeared on the horizon.

Badger said, "Maybe we should stay undercover."

They left the path and went into the woods.

Then Jack felt a hand around his mouth. A gun barrel stuck into his cheek.

A female voice said, "Don't shoot them."

The hand released.

Bebo stood in front them, pointing a sten gun. A man with long red hair and round spectacles was beside her.

Jack said, "I thought you were dead."

The young woman said, "We escaped and joined the Resistance. They found our foxhole last night."

Jonathan lay on a stretcher. His Royal Curfew uniform was covered in blood. There were bandages around his neck.

He looked up and said, "What are you doing here?"

"I escaped from a death camp."

"I'm surprised anyone bothered taking you prisoner."

Jack said, "I went through the Mouth."

"You've been through the Mouth?" the long-haired man said.

Jonathan snorted, "Don't encourage him, Canadian,"

"Now I need to get to London," Jack said.

"Well, you'd better come with us."

The group walked through the woods. The Canadian gestured at something ahead of them. They set the stretcher down behind a thorn bush and lay on the ground. Two Curfew soldiers walked past.

The Canadian gestured to move on.

The group followed the man to a copse of tall fir trees. The long-haired man knelt down and ran his hands over the forest floor. He found a length of rope and pulled it. A wooden hatch opened. It revealed a dark cavity.

The Canadian jumped inside and passed out a heavy canvas bag.

The group left the woods and walked over grassland to a wide estuary.

The beach defences left the coastline and continued along a metal bridge spanning the river before resuming their course on the other side.

They walked down to the shingle. There was a single automated Browning. The barrel was twisted out of shape.

The Canadian said, "This area is called Red Sands. A few years ago there was a massive storm that knocked out the beach defences, the inner wall and about a quarter of a mile of the outer wall. Weather seems to be the only thing that can make a dent in these things—the rockets won't launch against wind or rain."

Bebo said, "I think Jonathan is dead."

The Canadian said, "I'm sorry to hear that."

He unzipped the canvas bag and heaved out a black tube that slithered onto the pebbles. He unrolled it. A hard-bottomed boat deck unfolded inside an inflatable dinghy.

The long-haired man said, "Since the storm small objects can get through with a fair wind and a bit of luck."

Badger said, "Luck?"

"There are some heat-seeking torpedos about half a mile out. Type 48s. Some of them are still working."

The Canadian handed Badger a rubber foot pump and said, "Jack and Bebo get some branches from the wood. As thick as possible. We need to break up our heat patterns and try to fool the thermal sensors."

When they were in the trees Jack held up his hand and wiggled his new finger at Bebo.

She caught hold of his wrist and said, "That's impossible."

Bebo grabbed the back of his neck and held a knife to his throat.

"Who are you?" She said.

"I'm me."

"When we were children we swam in a stream. What grew on the banks?"

"Bamboo."

Bebo took the knife away. Then she hugged him.

He said, "I went to a different world. If I can do it again I may be able to hurt King Eustace."

"How?"

"I need to get to the Mouth. In London."

They collected branches and walked back to the beach.

Grey clouds were massing in the sky. Gusts of cold rain blew in from the sea.

The two men had donned metallic heat suits.

The Canadian said, "Anti-radar suits. Put them on."

Badger said, "I don't like the look of that sea, much."

The Canadian pulled the drawstring on his hood, leaving a small oval of white face.

"No, nor me," he said. "Anyone been on the water before?"

"We grew up next to a lake," Bebo said.

"Good. You two can row then."

Chapter Seventeen
The Fort

They laid Jonathan's body in the boat.

Bebo said, "Why are we taking him with us?"

"It might help explain any activity from the Sea Wall if a body washes up later."

The group held the dinghy over their heads and squeezed between the stubs of storm-damaged Q-Interceptor incendiary rockets.

Salt spray and rain pattered on the anti-radar suits as they stepped onto the shingle.

The Canadian said, "Keep an eye out for Hedgehog mines. A lot got washed away in the storm, but there's still a few around.

They splashed into the surf and waded out into hip-deep broken water.

The sea roared around them.

The Canadian climbed into the inflatable and squatted in the front while Badger went aft. They arranged the branches around themselves. Jack and Bebo set the oars in the locks and pulled.

When the dinghy was a few hundred yards out the Canadian said, "Okay, let's lose the body."

The group tipped Jonathan's corpse out of the dinghy.

Ahead of them rain stippled the surface of the dark water.

A helicopter flew across the estuary.

The Canadian said, "We've been compromised. They must be trying to figure out why the defences aren't deploying against us."

The flying machine swooped low over the marshland.

Badger said, "We're sitting ducks out here."

The Canadian said, "The sensors will detect their engine."

The helicopter flew over the beach.

Half a mile out to sea two white rockets detached from the outer Wall.

"Biddle 88 heat-seekers. This should be interesting."

The sleek missiles each described a semi circle in the air. The first one incinerated the helicopter and the second blew up the falling fuselage.

The long-haired man said, "Wow."

As they rowed out to the line of ballistic missiles the Canadian said, "The purple tubes holding up the Outer Sea wall are a mystery. I haven't found anyone who knows what they are composed of or who created them."

Ahead of them, the hole in the outer Sea Wall became visible. At the edges, ribbons of electrical wire and twisted metal twirled in the waves like seaweed. A half-submerged rocket bobbed up and down.

The Canadian said, "That one in the water is a 'Canterbury Fire-And-Forget Tactical Nuke.' You could take out half of America with just that single missile."

"There are sensors mounted on the sea bed underneath us. Each one is completely autonomous. No-one controls them, not even King Eustace himself. Each can independently launch anti-personnel, aerial and ship weapons."

Some colored lights lit up on a ruined section of the wall.

"The sensors here are all in bad shape. When they are damaged, they become conservative. If there is a nearby weapons launch, any sensor will shut down and reboot itself before firing at the same target. It's designed to stop them all attacking the same thing at once."

The Canadian took a red pistol from a plastic box and said, "I've worked out it takes four minutes before they relaunch. More than enough time for us to get through the hole in the outer Sea Wall."

He turned back towards the shore and fired the pistol. A bright white flare raced over the water before it pierced the surface of the sea and sank into the gloom.

A plume of white foam fizzed out from the area where the flare had disappeared. There was a massive boom and a wall of water rushed towards them.

The Canadian said, "Torpedo. Pull the oars in."

The dinghy rode the white crest of the first wave. The Canadian brought out a paddle and knelt at the prow frantically rowing so the boat pointed forwards. Then they were engulfed in surf as they surged through the sea wall.

Jack hung onto a grab rope on the side of the boat until the foaming water subsided. Then they were in open water.

The Canadian said, "We're still alive. Good. Badger and I can take our turn on the oars."

The waves grew bigger, the rise and fall more pronounced. Soon they were rowing amongst dark hills of massing water.

The Canadian stopped to take out a plastic compass and look at the horizon.

"Are you really Canadian?" Jack said.

The Canadian winked.

"Don't tell anyone. I'm actually French. My name is Kempthorne. I am a descendant of British refugees who were on holiday in France."

A group of silhouetted shapes appeared on the horizon.

As the boat got nearer the indistinct forms coalesced into square buildings sitting on top of high concrete legs.

Bebo said, "What are they?"

Kempthorne said, "They were built to defend the coast during the Second World War and then abandoned. They had anti-aircraft guns on the top of them. The one in the middle is the command tower. That's where we're going."

They rowed over. The stilts rose seventy feet out of the water. The squat box above them was made of riveted sheet metal that was orange with rust.

The Canadian tied the dinghy to a silver-coloured platform that looked newer than the building high above it.

"Leave your guns in the boat. We'll be watched."

The speedboat at the far end of the walkway had a raised cockpit. GENDARMERIE MARITIME was painted in black letters on a sleek grey hull.

The Canadian stopped by a central ladder and climbed up.

A circular hatch led into a derelict room that was thick with rust. Wind whistled through broken glass in the portholes. The bitumen deck was thick with bird droppings.

A ladder in the corner led up to a large, warm room that had naval charts along the walls. An outsize plotting table was covered in maps.

The Canadian said, "This is where the fun starts."

A man with a big, unshaven face emerged from a side room. He wore a black turtle-necked jumper. His dark eyes darted between the visitors.

A young man and woman appeared behind him. They both had spiky blonde hair and matching silver nose-rings.

The Canadian turned to the others and said, "This gentleman is called Pompey. He's in charge here. Octavia and Constantine are his crew. They are twins."

Pompey said something in French.

The Canadian said, "In English please, mon Commandant. I've brought some friends from the mainland."

"Strangers are not allowed here."

"The foxhole was discovered. Cartwright was killed. I had no choice."

"And the explosions?"

"A helicopter."

"So you have alerted the British authorities to our presence out here."

"These people have vital intelligence. They would have been killed."

"Are you familiar with King Eustace's last recorded message that he will respond to any incursion on mainland Britain with a nuclear strike?"

"He can't launch anything. The system is automated."

"We don't know that."

A flash of orange light shone through the windows. There was a far-off boom.

"I have been able to confirm the existence of a powerful device known as the Mouth," the Canadian said.

"The magic machine. The British government-in-exile doesn't believe that story. Nor does the Swimming Pool in Paris."

"Nothing else could explain how King Eustace did what he did."

"Have you seen this machine yourself?"

"No."

"You've been in the field far too long. Michel for once in your life, listen. There is a hole in the Great Patriotic Sea Wall now. We think Eustace Champion has lost the means to repair it. We need to patiently build up intelligence and find some way to liberate the country without starting a third world war."

The Canadian said, "We can't just wait for more freak weather to knock the wall down. There are death camps in England and Scotland. People who need saving now, not in a hundred years time."

Pompey said, "Lieutenant Kempthorne I am placing you under arrest. Your English friends are going to get in the dinghy and row back to the mainland. You will come with us. We are evacuating this fort."

Kempthorne pointed an automatic pistol at Pompey.

He said, "Badger, Bebo take their guns, if anyone moves, shoot them. Because believe me, they will shoot you. Jack, come with me."

They climbed a metal ladder to the next floor, which was filled with outsize plastic water containers and cardboard storage boxes.

The Canadian opened a door into a thin room with a long rack of clothes. He selected two dark suits, white shirts and underwear and took two shoeboxes from a pile in the corner.

He said, "You're about the same size as Cartwright. He would have agreed with what I'm doing."

They took off their sodden clothes.

Kempthorne buckled a skin-coloured canvas belt around Jack's chest and wrapped one around himself.

Jack put on his clothes and said, "Why the red waistcoats?"

"Where we are going servants wear them. We will be servants among other servants."

He took out two round cardboard boxes and put them into plastic bags.

"It's a gated holiday village called Haven—a reward for the sociopaths who collaborate with King Eustace's regime."

They went back into the storage room. Kempthorne took Jack's photograph with a mobile telephone. A nearby printer whirred into action.

"Our cover story is that we are on a day trip buying fish to take back to our employers in London."

He took papers from the printer and shoved them into Jack's jacket pockets.

"The tricky part will be obtaining a pass to travel through the actual London wall. They call it an Ostium. You can only get one when you are inside Haven. King Eustace is paranoid. We'll have to improvise."

A wooden weapons rack was propped up against a wall beside a wooden crate marked EXPLOSIF.

Kempthorne unlocked the rack and took out two automatic pistols.

"These are plastic Glocks, courtesy of the Swimming Pool in Paris—French Naval Intelligence. They won't show up in a metal detector. There is a pocket in the belt—"

Kempthorne pulled Jack's shirt back and holstered the pistol between his shoulder blades.

"Hopefully they won't pat us down there. If you get caught with a weapon it's summary execution, of course."

Kempthorne stowed his own gun and took four cakes of explosive from the crate. He loosened his shirt and put two in the under-arm pockets of the skin-coloured belt. Jack copied him.

"They have a thirty second fuse. Pull the plastic ring pull and stand well back."

He handed Jack a wad of money and two flat tins with RATION DE COMBAT ARMEE FRANCAIS printed on the side.

"French cooking. Don't get caught with them. Our contact is a fisherwoman called Hobsbawne. She has good reason to hate the King. Let's put our anti-radar suits back on."

As they climbed down the Canadian said, "I never asked you, where are we going when we get to London?"

"Buckingham Palace."

Kempthorne laughed and said, "Of course, where else?"

Badger said, "Pompey has offered us a cushy life in France if we give you up."

"I'm glad you didn't take him up on it. Get down the ladder and keep your gun on these three."

When they were in the derelict room Kempthorne picked an iron bar off the floor and said to Pompey, "We're taking the speedboat."

"Michel, don't be an idiot," Pompey said.

Badger opened the hatch. Bebo climbed down.

Pompey said, "You are risking the destruction of the entire planet."

Jack followed Badger down the ladder. Kempthorne followed and jammed the metal opening shut with the iron bar.

As they descended, a distant light blinked in the sky.

Jack ran along the metal platform.

Kempthorne ripped a tarpaulin cover from the back of the speedboat.

Bebo and Badger climbed onboard while Jack tethered the inflatable dinghy to the boat.

The lights in the elevated steel building went out.

The twins jumped out of a high window.

Kempthorne climbed into the boat and said, "Come on.

The helicopter was almost overhead now, whipping spray into their eyes.

Kempthorne started the boat's engine.

Pompey opened a door in the side of the old tower. He raised a high calibre rifle and took aim at the speedboat.

The bullet smashed through the cockpit's front window. A cloud of blood puffed out behind Lieutenant Kempthorne's heart.

He looked at Jack for a second, as if he was thinking, and said, "I am shot."

Then his eyes rolled back.

An amplified voice from the helicopter said, "You are in British territorial waters. Drop your weapons and put your hands behind your heads or we will open fire."

The twins pulled themselves onto the metal gangway and unzipped two waterproof bags.

Octavia pointed a sniper's rifle at the speedboat.

A searchlight swept the old fort and settled on Pompey. The helicopter turned to face him. A bright rope of liquid orange flame shot out of the flying machine and engulfed the Commandant.

Octavia turned her gun on the helicopter. She was caught in the spotlight and a red hole appeared above her left eyebrow. She crumpled and splashed back into the water.

Constantine shot at the flying machine. An answering bullet knocked him into the water.

Bright orange light flickered in the metal tower's windows. The fire reached the EXPLOSIF boxes. A massive ball of flame blew the old metal building open and knocked the enemy war machine out of the sky.

Jack watched the helicopter fall sideways into the water. A wall of noise and heat roared over them and knocked the speedboat on one side. Jack was in the freezing water for a second before the vessel righted itself.

Badger floated face down in knee-deep seawater. Jack propped him up on one of the leather seats that lined the boat.

Pieces of burning paper drifted in the air. A map with the title UN PLAN DE BOURNEMOUTH fluttered past the cockpit.

Badger coughed out blood and teeth.

The front of the building had folded open like a sardine tin. Black smoke poured out. The concrete stilts underneath the metal fort were skewed to one side.

A pair of hands threw two oars into the speedboat. Bebo hauled herself out of the water.

Jack went into the boat's cockpit and studied a computer display above the wheel. There was a line representing the sea wall. Beneath it a red dot flashed on and off.

Bebo put her hand on Jack's shoulder.

He said, "It's a map showing the sea wall. The dot is us."

There was a rending sound behind them as the burning tower sunk into the sea.

Jack gunned the engine. The speedboat roared over the water.

Badger said, "The gavvers will be waiting for us."

Jack said, "The radio is always jammed along the coast. That might help."

"We could go to France, come back when things have calmed down," Badger said.

Jack watched the flashing red dot get nearer to the line.

Bebo said, "What did the Canadian say to you?"

"He had a plan."

"I want to be part of it. I'm not leaving you. I'm a soldier for freedom now."

"You need an identity card to go where I'm going."

Jack switched the engine off and said, "My chances are pretty slim. I'll probably end up like the grandpa, Dad, Amy, Ann, Jonathan and all the rest of them. But I'm going anyway."

Bebo said, "You sound like a different person."

"I have been reborn more than once."

Jack dropped into the dinghy and said, "I hope you both have a good life in France."

Bebo passed him the oars.

Badger said, "Bon chance, mate."

Jack rowed towards the coast and did not look back.

Chapter Eighteen
"The All-Year-Round Oompah Band"

Surf roared between the purple tubes that held up the Great Patriotic Sea Wall.

Jack tied the dinghy to the fin of a missile snagged in the wreckage at the edge of the storm breach.

He climbed up onto the launching ledge. The smooth shelf was made from the same ageless material as the beams and the Mouth.

He sat down. Blinking letters appeared on the surface next to him. They said, PROXIMITY DETECTION. There was a grating sound. A metal panel half-opened above his shoulder. A rusty hypodermic syringe emerged and made a sucking sound before dropping onto the bench and rolling into the sea. The little hatch tried to close but got stuck half way down.

Jack could see people on the path studying the smoking remains of two crashed helicopters on the beach. They were looking through binoculars and not risking the danger from any sentry guns or Hedgehog mines lying in the shingle.

He took a tin from his pocket. The label said, NAVINE D'AGNEAU. It had a ring pull.

He ate a mouthful and said, "Lamb stew. Cheers Michel."

Then he closed his eyes.

When he woke there was a single soldier watching over the burned helicopters.

The moon was bright.

Jack rowed the dinghy into an area of dark shadow cast by a cliff behind the beach.

There were no Type 48 torpedos this time.

There was a body lying at the edge of the water. Jonathan's oiled side parting and pencil-thin moustache still looked impeccably groomed. One of his eyes was half open and stared up at the moon.

Jack splashed into the freezing surf and dragged the dinghy onto the pebbles.

A Browning sentry gun rose out of the shingle and made clicking sounds.

Jack rolled his brother's body into the dinghy and took off his anti-radar suit. Then he pushed the boat into the surf and threw the oars after it.

Jack took the raincoat out of the plastic bag and opened the round box. It contained a bowler hat.

He put it on.

Then he pulled the documents from his jacket and held them up to the moonlight. A blue identity card said EUSTACE HOBSBAWNE. INDENTURED SERVANT. There was a CURFEW VISA. The third piece of paper was a map covered in Kempthorne's handwriting.

The soldier on the beach had gone.

He met with no-one as he walked along the path behind the seashore.

The sky had lightened to a gunmetal grey when he found the signpost saying DYMGATE. The path to the village was half-hidden in fireweed bushes.

A white pub was the only building untouched by fire. A sign hanging outside said THE LORD NELSON.

There was a wooden hatch in the pavement underneath. He pulled it open and swung down into the darkness.

The little damp room smelt foul. The bicycles were where Kempthorne's notes had written they would be— behind two empty beer barrels.

A hand grabbed Jack's ankle. He lost his balance and his head hit the stone floor.

Then he felt a heavy body on top of him. An arm pushed against his windpipe. He kneed his attacker between the legs and the pressure faltered. He did it again and the body rolled off him.

Jack searched the floor for his bowler hat.

He said, "I've got a gun."

No one answered. He pushed one of the bicycles through the hatch and climbed out after it.

There was a long line of abandoned cars outside the town. Moss had colonized the old tarmac road.

Soon he was in the countryside, cycling past fields of winter rye and overgrown meadows.

In the early afternoon, he sat on a birch tree that had fallen across the road.

The black lettering on his last tin of food said, CASSOULET SUPERIERE AU CONFIT DE CANARD.

A small girl appeared behind him. She wore a dress made of rabbit skins. Her hand grabbed at the food.

Jack said, "Let's share it."

He ate half and offered her the tin.

She took it and then snapped her thumb against her palm. It was a Curfew gesture that meant man-traps were nearby.

He looked around. There was a circle of serrated steel in the grass beside the exposed roots of the fallen birch.

He said, "Thanks," and made the Curfew salute of the index finger against the nose.

The girl returned the salute and disappeared into the bushes.

Jack got back on his bicycle.

The town of Haven was encircled by a high brick wall topped with broken glass.

Jack looked at his map. Kempthorne had written SERVANT'S ENTRANCE and drawn an arrow pointing to the South West of the wall.

A Centurion tank stood beside an ornate iron gate. A sign above the entrance way said, SERVICE IS ITS OWN REWARD.

Three members of the Royal Curfews warmed their hands over a brazier full of burning coal. Their battle dress uniforms were patched and dirty.

Jack cycled up and said, "Good afternoon, gentlemen."

One of the men turned. His two front teeth were missing.

He said, "Papers."

His breath smelled of fish. Jack handed his identity card over.

"Curfew Visa?"

Jack gave it to him.

The soldier said, "Why are you travelling outside Haven?"

"My employers were kind enough to give me the afternoon off. I wanted to enjoy the fresh air."

"Did you indeed? Arms up."

The man patted him down and said, "All right. On your toes."

He wheeled his bike through the gate.

A dirt road took him to the sea front.

An expanse of wet sand reflected the setting sun.

There were no missiles on the beach here.

The murderous line out to sea was still there, although so far out as to be almost invisible.

A shire horse pulled a wooden cart with CAPPIN AND SON SHRIMPS written on the side. It dragged a ten-foot-wide trawl net through the shallow water.

Dozens of wooden fishing boats bobbed amongst glittering waves.

Jack cycled past some old stone huts along the sea front.

He went down a hill.

A sign said, WORKERS VILLAGE.

He got off his bike in a muddy courtyard surrounded by tall houses. The buildings had once been painted in garish colours that were now dulled by grime.

There was a grinny pole in the middle of the yard. A man wearing a flat cap was leaning against it.

Two children threw stones at each other.

Jack walked up to the man and said, "I wonder if you could help me. I'm looking for Mrs Hobsbawne."

The man looked at him impassively.

He said, "What do you want with her?"

"She's my aunt."

"I haven't seen you before."

"No, it's my first time in Haven."

"Third floor in the yellow building. You shouldn't go around asking questions. You'll get in trouble."

Jack went into the building, climbed three flights of stairs and knocked.

He said, "Hello? Mrs Hobsbawne? It's your nephew, Eustace."

A door opened half an inch. A woman with white hair and mottled skin stared through the gap.

Jack said, "The Canadian sent me."

The door opened.

The little room had bare floorboards. An old double mattress leant against a wall.

Two crates stood on either side of a metal stove.

Mrs Hobsbawne stirred a cooking pot with a wooden spoon and said, "Where are you from?"

"The Curfew."

"You don't look like a cave man."

"No."

"The Canadian never mentioned you."

"The Canadian is dead."

She stopped stirring and said, "Oh. How?"

"He was shot. He didn't suffer much. Do you live on your own here?"

"My husband had emphysema. They said it was an apocryphal sickness belief. It wasn't. He died."

"I need to get into London."

"You'll need an Ostium. They use fingerprints and eye scans."

"Yes. How do I get one?"

"From the Transport Office in Freedom Square. But they only issue them to employers—who buy them on behalf of their servants. You'll have to find some other way."

"Yes."

Mrs. Hobsbawne poured white stew onto two plates.

They sat on the crates. The white-haired woman ripped a slice of bread in half and handed him a piece.

"I feel bad eating your food," Jack said

"What are we put on this earth for, if not to help each other?"

"You sound like my grandpa."

Afterwards the old lady washed the plates in a basin.

She dropped the mattress onto the floor and said, "I have an early start."

Mrs Hobsbawne lay down. Jack put his gun into his hat and placed them on the floor. He got in beside her. The old woman blew out the candle.

She said, "Helping the Canadian is the only thing that has kept me going. I killed someone myself once, during the famine of 96. There were bodies on the streets. People started eating each other. The King said malnutrition and hunger were the result of apocryphal mental beliefs, not because there was no food. They sent a soldier out with each boat to make sure we didn't steal the catch. David would sometimes hide a couple of codling in his pocket. This soldier caught him and started beating him to death with his rifle. I grabbed a filleting knife and stuck it into the back of his neck. We pushed him over the side. When we got back no-one even noticed. He was a Curfew soldier."

Jack said, "Thank you for helping me."

He slept until a hand shook him awake. It was still dark outside.

They joined a throng of men and women streaming out of the slum buildings in the Worker's Village.

She said, "I'm going to my boat. Good luck, I hope you make it."

Jack queued at a check point for workers entering the holiday resort.

He eventually went through the rectangular frame of a walk-through metal detector. It was called the RADIO INVESTIGATOR. A female technician sitting beside it listened impassively to a pair of headphones.

There were half a dozen officials wearing the oversized white peaked caps and gold epaulettes of the Royal People's Army dress uniform. Red truncheons hung from their wrists.

An elderly man studied Jack's face.

He said, "Got any fags or sweeties on you?"

"No."

"Make sure you get something for me next time. I'll remember your face."

A second guard patted him down.

A German Shepherd dog sniffed around him.

The workers entered a stone courtyard that had different paths leading off it.

There was a notice board with a SERVANTS MAP on it. Jack studied it.

He cycled up a road carved from a chalk cliff.

There were railings on the side overlooking the sea.

A group of children played cricket on the beach.

When he got to RESPONSIBILITY SQUARE his wheels juddered so badly he had to get off his bicycle.

He bent down to look at the ground. The square was cobbled with human skulls. They were preserved in a hard see-through resin. A few lay on their side, showing eye sockets and jawbones.

Colourful bunting hung between ornate lamp posts.

There was a bandstand in the middle of the square. THE ALL-YEAR-ROUND OOMPAH BRASS BAND was painted on a wooden cupola. Men and women in brightly colored uniforms were getting into position.

Beyond it the stalls of the fishmongers were already busy. Child apprentices wheeled barrows of fish on beds of ice. Fishmongers chalked up the prices for today's catch.

There was a FISH AND CHIPS shop and a PRINCE AUGUSTINE PUB. A striped pole twirled above a BARBER SHOP offering HAIRCUTS FOR 3/6.

Jack walked up to the ROYAL PIER and watched the wooden fishing boats.

In the bandstand, a woman wearing a red tailcoat held up a conductors baton. A stocky man with a walrus moustache banged on a big drum. The band blew into gleaming brass instruments.

Jack was the only audience.

Fishmongers started to shout their prices.

Then Jack saw a man wearing a red waistcoat and bowler hat cycle up to a fish stall.

The servant had a thin face and a square tuft of beard under his lower lip. He watched carefully as fish were placed in white boxes and handed to him.

Jack walked over to the stalls.

An apprentice shouted, "Soles, bass, plaice, whiting, all fresh sir."

Jack turned and said, "Six plaice, please."

The boy handed him a box. Jack passed the boy a pound note and said, "Keep it."

The apprentice gave a small bow.

The servant with the square tuft of beard got onto his bicycle and pedalled across the square.

Jack waited a few seconds before following him over the skull cobbles.

The servant turned into a tree-lined avenue that was surrounded by expensive-looking villas.

There was a sign by a hump-backed bridge that said, CANAL CROSSING. The waterway beneath it was frozen.

The servant cycled over it and turned into CHILDERNESSE LANE.

The houses here were hidden from the road by tall cypress hedges.

Jack followed the man up a gravel path to a driveway outside a mock-Tudor manor house.

The servant was packing boxes of fish into the boot of a white Rolls Royce.

Jack rode up and said, "Excuse me, sir?"

The man turned.

Jack said, "I wonder if I could beg a moment of your time. The car I intended to drive to London in has broken down."

"Yes?"

"I wonder if I might prevail upon you to give me a lift into town? I would pay you for your trouble, of course."

Jack reached into his shirt and pulled out a roll of bank notes.

The servant waved a hand and said, "I can't help you. You will have to telephone your employers and arrange a replacement."

"This is a lot of money."

The man smiled and said, "It wouldn't be much use to me hanging from a grinny. Now whatever you are up to, get lost."

Jack reached between his shoulder blades and pulled the plastic Glock out.

"I'm afraid I must insist," he said.

Chapter Nineteen
Mr. Parks

The servant put Jack's bicycle into the boot of the vintage car.

Jack opened the passenger door and said, "Don't try anything."

A faint odour of lemon-scented air freshener came out of the Rolls Royce.

They sat on either side of a cream-coloured leather seat.

The servant drove them along a tree-lined avenue and said, "My father was in the Resistance."

"Good for him."

They passed a group of men in fur coats playing golf on an immaculate green.

Jack said, "What's your name?"

"Mr Parks."

The Rolls Royce drove through an arched gateway in the high town wall.

A signpost said, THANK YOU FOR VISITING HAVEN. PROUD TO BE A DISEASE-FREE AREA.

They drove up to a wooden hut. A soldier with an outsize peaked cap flicked a cigarette through a kiosk window. It bounced off the car's windscreen.

"I presume you have a Curfew Visa?" Mr Parks said.

Jack gave it to him.

Mr Parks wound down the window and held out the two pieces of paper. The soldier looked at them, wrote something in a book and handed them back.

The arm of a metal barrier swung upwards.

Concrete walls on both sides of the motorway hid the countryside.

Jack said, "I have to get into London. I don't have an Ostium to get through the wall."

"I can't help you. It's completely impossible. They use biometrics to scan your eyes and fingerprints. I've already been through re-education. It nearly killed me. I won't do it again."

"I have explosives. Is there any way I can blow it up?"

"What? No, of course not. The wall is hundreds of feet thick."

"Try and think of a way to get me through."

They drove in silence for a while. Mr Parks lit a WOODBINE cigarette with a gold-plated lighter and said, "The London wall needs power to run. It used to be self-sufficient but they couldn't replace the solar panels. A lot of the electricity is supplied by coal-fired power stations. King Eustace doesn't like big loads going through the wall so the power plants were built out here in the Curfew. All of the power is routed through substations."

"So?"

"Before I was re-educated I was in the Royal Engineers. If we get inside a substation there are things I could do to close it down."

"What would that do?"

"The Peace Wall would shut down for miles."

Mr Parks jerked the steering wheel and the Rolls Royce skidded through a hole in the barrier.

"Motorway maintenance," he said.

They drove through an abandoned Curfew village and turned onto a tarmac road.

Mr Parks stopped the car and said, "Lose the waistcoat and hat."

They walked up an overgrown path towards a chain link fence. A triangular sign on an entrance gate said, DANGER OF DEATH. KEEP OUT.

Jack holstered the Glock between his shoulder blades.

A young Royal Curfew Regiment soldier slept on a chair behind the gate. His beret was pulled low over his eyes and he had wrapped himself in an oil-stained tarpaulin.

Behind him there was a compound filled with electrical machinery.

An older soldier with oiled hair walked towards them. The arm of his padded camouflaged jacket had three stripes on it.

He said, "Good morning gentlemen. This is an unexpected surprise."

The younger soldier stood up and the tarpaulin fell to the floor. He was cradling a Sterling sub-machine gun in his arms.

Mr Parks said, "Morning sergeant. Ministry of Works. Spot check. We are looking for vulnerabilities to terrorist attack."

The older soldier said, "No-one told us."

"It wouldn't be much of a surprise inspection if anyone had."

The man looked at Jack and said, "Who are you?"

"He's my son. I've just picked him up from the Children's Palace."

"You're a very lucky young man to be studying there."

"He will be better able to serve our beloved leader."

The sergeant stood to attention and opened the gate. He said, "Long live King Eustace."

"Good man. I'll start with the Control Room."

They followed the soldier past bays of dirty machinery. They went into a square concrete building. The walls were covered in metal cabinets and dials.

There was a narrow window opposite the entrance. The glass was caked with dirt.

The sergeant sat down in a wooden chair in the corner of the room. A metal fire bucket beside him was brimming with cigarette butts. He propped his Lee Enfield rifle against a wall.

Mr Parks took a clipboard that hung from a hook and leafed through a few sheets of paper.

Then he rummaged in a metal tool box and took out a heavy spanner.

He brought it down on the soldier's nose. The man cried out and fell onto the floor, clutching his face.

Mr Parks picked up the Sergeants' rifle and worked the bolt.

The door opened.

The younger soldier stood in the doorway. He raised his submachine gun.

Mr Parks put a bullet in his chest.

The older soldier grabbed Mr Parks' legs.

The servant twisted his body and shot the man in the back of the head.

Then Mr Parks turned the gun on Jack.

There was silence for a few seconds.

Mr Parks lowered the Enfield.

He opened a panel on one of the metal cabinets and pulled a lever.

"I'll start an arcing fault. The main transformer is insulated with oil. Switch off the circuit breakers and the high voltage will boil it. The transformer will vent clouds of oil. The arcing electricity will ignite the cloud and blow this place sky high. I hope. Get ready to run."

He flicked some switches.

A high-pitched electrical hum sounded behind the back wall. Blue light flickered in the narrow window.

Mr Parks threw another switch and said, "Don't touch anything on your way out."

They ran through the substation. A bright blue arc of electricity danced around the bays roasting any machines in its path.

The flames began to alternate blue and yellow, lighting up the smoke billowing through the compound.

As they ran out of the gate the substation blew up.

Both of them were thrown forward into the grass and showered with chunks of smoking masonry.

Jack felt the hair on the back of his head shrivel as waves of heat passed over them.

The smoke blinded him and he closed his eyes. When he opened them Mr Parks was firing the Sterling into the burning compound, laughing with delight.

When he finished they got back into the Rolls Royce and continued up the tarmac road.

The wall crept up the horizon.

Mr Parks parked the Rolls Royce in a car park at the foot of the massive smooth-skinned London wall.

Half a dozen cars were parked in front of a glass building that said BIOMETRICS. A crowd of Royal Protection Agency soldiers stood outside.

The entrance to the tunnel was blocked by a purple mesh.

Jack held out a wad of bank notes and said, "Please take this. You've earned it."

Mr Parks accepted the money and smiled. He pulled Jack's bicycle from the boot of the car and fixed an electric torch between the handlebars.

"You'll need that where you are going," he said.

Mr Parks put Jack's box of plaice in the wicker basket.

They walked to a small red door beside the tunnel entrance.

A sign said, SOUTH GATE SERVICE ACCESS. HAND IN FOOTWEAR.

"The door to the service tunnel is six feet on your right as you walk in. It should be open. You picked the right man to kidnap," he said.

They went inside.

It was dark.

A voice said, "Who is there?"

Mr Parks coughed a few times while Jack carried his bicycle through a door.

As it closed behind him he saw the guard light a match. The flame illuminated a small room. A member of the Royal People's Army stood in front of a rack of shoes. Mr Parks raised his bowler hat.

Jack switched the bicycle light on.

The service tunnel was only a few feet wide.

A line of glass on the right hand side of the passage overlooked the empty vehicle tunnel.

A mass of cables ran along the top of the ceiling.

He got on his bicycle and pedalled.

His coat brushed against the wall.

He saw something ahead of him and stopped. It was a black metal box with an almost human-shaped head. A single eye in the forehead seemed to be observing the vehicle tunnel through the long window.

There were presences like this every few hundred feet.

Then a square of light appeared in the distance.

He saw a figure lean out of a booth.

A voice said, "Who is that? Simon?"

Jack switched his light off and pedaled hard. A hand grabbed at his arm as he swept past, but it was not quick enough.

Chapter Twenty
A Delivery

The access door to the service tunnel was unlocked. Jack's bicycle juddered down concrete steps. Then he was out in the open air. No one in the queue of vehicles waiting for the tunnel tried to stop him.

He cycled along a fenced-in road between a vast shantytown of wooden huts.

The shacks gave way to terraced houses whose bomb-damaged roofs and blown-out windows were patched up with plywood and corrugated iron.

By mid-morning he was passing towering housing blocks that were connected together by walkways hundreds of feet in the air.

He cycled over WESTMINSTER BRIDGE.

Two sculptures of raised Lee Enfield rifles crossed to form an arch over TRAFALGAR SQUARE. There were no fountains or Christmas tree. Bodies hung from grinnies in each corner.

Four Centurions were parked in the middle of the paving stones. The tank captains stood behind front-mounted high-calibre machine guns.

A sculpture of King Eustace stood on top of Nelson's column wearing the admiral's clothes. The brass lions of the other world had been replaced by giant sculptures of the King's favourite dogs.

Jack cycled past a row of empty shops and wheeled his bicycle at a railway station.

He bought a cup of tea and an iced bun at a LYONS CAFÉ. He sat on a bench opposite a glass display cabinet called the MUSEUM OF DISCREDITED MEDICINE. It was full of surgical instruments with painted-on blood.

Scores of travelers looked up at a display showing train times to the walled factory towns of the North.

He gazed at the ceiling. There was a painting of King Eustace directing war machines at the battle of Oxford using a touch screen computer.

Jack got up and studied a wall map of the local area.

Then he got on his bike and cycled up Grosvenor Place.

There was a wall around Buckingham Palace. The tops of plane trees in the palace garden rocked gently in the wind.

He went up Constitution Hill. A side entrance was protected by a soldier who sat behind a belt-fed Lewis machine gun propped up on a wall of sandbags.

He stopped a few hundred yards further up the hill in front of a wooden gate set in the outside wall. It had two doors. A sign said VEHICLE ACCESS ONLY.

Jack unbuttoned his shirt and took out a cake of explosive. He moulded the black putty around the gate's lock and yanked the plastic ring-pull.

Then he crossed the road.

The shockwave knocked him into the bushes.

One door was blown off its hinges. The other swung backwards.

He put his bowler hat back on, held up his box of plaice and walked through the burning gates.

Jack tried a few windows along the east wing of the palace until he found one that pulled up.

The state room was full of Chinese porcelain.

He opened an avocado-coloured door. Two Royal Political agents ran past.

Jack walked out into a long corridor.

A blonde woman ran out of an office and said, "What is all the fuss about?"

He said, "There's a fire. Someone should call the fire brigade."

A man in a red waistcoat heard him and unlocked a glass-fronted fire hose cabinet. Keys hung off his belt.

Jack held his plastic Glock beneath the fish box and said, "Take me to King Eustace's private office or I will shoot you."

They walked up the corridor. The servant stopped outside an oak door.

Jack said, "Open it. Hurry."

Another Royal Political agent ran past. The man unlocked the door.

Jack handed the box of fish to the servant.

"Leave the keys and get lost," he said.

The Mouth sat in the corner of a wood-panelled office.

He stuck a chair under the door handle.

There was a beige computer on the desk beside the device.

Jack pressed a key on a keyboard.

Someone said, "Get this door open."

The display said PASSWORD?

He typed VAE VICTIS.

Then the voice of King Eustace came through the door, "Is that my friend Jack? You are a very resourceful young man. Open the door and I can promise you that you will get a jolly good hearing. I encourage debate. I don't mind people criticizing me as long as they get the facts right."

The computer display said ENTER CO-ORDINATES.

Jack typed [a81/05/71] [68/9017].

The Mouth seemed to stir. The purple basin rotated a few degrees.

Champion's voice said, "I went where the evidence led me. The best people say the trials I design are beautiful. Just beautiful."

Jack unbuttoned his shirt and searched the canvas belt for something that Mrs Hobsbawne had given him. He took out a tin of TORCH TOBACCO. The little mouse inside bit his index finger.

He placed it on the bowl and said, "Sorry old boy."

The King shouted, "Open the door you beastly fellow."

A gun fired. A bullet hole appeared in the door. The missile glanced off Jack's shoulder, spinning him around.

An arch of glistening pink flesh described a perfect curve over the bowl.

He slapped the second explosive charge onto the beige computer and yanked the plastic ring pull.

The black cake made a fizzing sound.

Someone charged the door. The hinges splintered.

Jack jumped into the Mouth.

Part IV, The Maximum

Chapter Twenty-One
The City of Yes-No

Fierce light from the explosion blazed somewhere behind him. Fifty years passed. Or that was what it felt like. Day after day. Mornings, afternoons, dark nights. Lessening him. No pity. Disconnected. Alone. He tried hard to remember himself and what he meant. And then there was the nothing of death. And then—

Jack fell into a puddle of water. Some went into his mouth. It was lukewarm and tasted of earth. He spat it out.

He rolled onto his back and looked up at the Mouth. The column and bowl were hidden under a thick layer of moss and lichen.

There was no roof above him. The rain that fell on his face was warm. The air was hot.

The walls were ruined and only a few feet high but it was King Eustace's office.

People had fought here. Spent cartridge cases lay amongst a few rotten scraps of carpet. There were high caliber bullet holes in the rain-blackened wood paneling.

He stood up.

A high-explosive shell had obliterated the entire east Wing of the Palace. There was a huge crater. The hole had filled with water and now knotted tree roots and ferns fringed a stagnant lake whose surface was covered in giant water lilies.

Palm trees grew out of smashed up masonry and earth. There were bright purple orchids and bowl-shaped plants with red petals and thick, waxy leaves.

A voice came across the water.

"I'm afraid you have to go back."

Jack walked to the edge of the depression.

He saw the far-off silhouette of a man sitting on a horse. The animal and its rider were framed in the doorway of a surviving wall.

The figure said, "We warned King Eustace."

"I have nothing to do with him. I am his enemy."

Jack watched the stranger ride around the crater lake.

The man wore blue jeans and a brown leather waistcoat. His arms were bare. His skin was black and his beard covered his chest. He rested a shotgun on one hip.

"Millions of people are dead," Jack said.

The chestnut-coloured horse came to a halt in front of Jack.

The man jumped down.

"I won't go back until I find out who gave King Eustace his power. You'll have to kill me.

The man stroked his beard. It gave off a smell of beeswax.

"My name is Aaron. My horse won't mind carrying both of us," he said.

Aaron climbed back in the saddle. Jack put his foot in the stirrup and swung up behind him.

They rode slowly around the lake.

The doorway in the surviving wall led into the Palace's central quadrangle. It was a mass of green foliage and coloured petals. The tail rotor of a crashed helicopter stuck out of a poinsettia bush.

They rode through the hallway of a pulverized building.

The Palace gardens were thick with exotic trees. The sun was bright and the air humid.

Jack said, "Why is it so hot?"

Aaron did not answer.

They crossed through a v-shaped opening in the half-collapsed palace boundary wall.

The road outside was wide and ruined. The big buildings on either side were empty shells hollowed out by aerial bombardment and ancient battle.

Aaron took them past a long pile of honey-coloured rubble.

They walked up Westminster Bridge. It had been blown up and the middle was missing. The horse walked to the edge.

Below them, an aircraft carrier lay on the riverbank. The hull was brown with rust. Acacia trees sprouted between the abandoned fighter jets on the ship's deck.

A movement in the sky caught Jack's eye. Something flew overhead, hundreds of feet up. It was a bubble of clear liquid. There was no engine noise but the slipstream threw up high crests of water in the Thames. Jack followed the progress of the craft until it disappeared into an entirely new city on the horizon.

There were hundreds of brightly colored structures made from the same smooth indestructible matter as the Mouth.

Most were egg-shaped or box-like. A few resembled pyramids. Steam came out of holes in their roofs.

Four black tube-shaped buildings towered above the city. They were thousands of storeys high and had windows that shimmered and rippled like water.

On the ground, coils and wires lay amongst the rubble of the destroyed city.

A slender white horizontal line lit up, suddenly connecting the city with the clouds.

"What is that?"

Aaron laughed. "That, if you can believe it, is an elevator to the moon," he said.

A trickle of sweat ran down Jack's back.

Aaron turned the horse around. Ahead of them a half-transparent yellow sphere hovered above what had once been Hyde Park.

The horse galloped between broken masonry and the clumps of palm and bamboo that grew along the river bank.

Aaron took them through a ruined ornamental garden that led into a clearing.

There was a wooden cabin built with uncut reddish-brown mahogany logs. It had a front porch. A rocking chair stood beside an electric fan.

Aaron went inside. Jack's mount lowered its neck and ate some grass.

Aaron trotted out from behind the cabin on a white horse.

He rode up to Jack and said, "It's too dangerous to stay around here. Your presence isn't welcome I'm afraid. Where are you from?"

"The Curfew."

"Where's that?"

"Placebo Sector 484. It used to be called Maidstone before it was burned down."

"Come on. Let's get out of here."

They rode along deserted streets.

By mid-day, they were out of the ruined city and galloping through an alien forest in the sweltering heat.

Later in the afternoon, the cover of the forest canopy gave way to open grassland.

Lukewarm rain pattered on Jack's bowler hat.

A flock of black birds swooped in a circle overhead and then dived at them.

Aaron fired his shotgun in the air. The birds squawked and scattered.

They rode up to a tall bridge. An old four-lane roadway was held up by cables that were suspended from towering pylons.

The riverbank on the other side was swathed in mist.

A concrete sign said QUEEN ELIZABETH II BRIDGE 1987.

Jack said, "No King Eustace here."

They galloped across the bridge.

The wind that sang in the long cables abruptly turned cold.

The rain transformed into icy flakes.

Half way along the bridge a line of white snow suddenly appeared on the tarmac ahead of them.

Aaron opened a saddlebag and handed Jack a fur-lined jacket and a pair of woollen gloves.

He said, "Put these on."

They galloped over the white downs in the fading light of a low winter sun.

Jack said, "This is the Weald."

"Yes."

There was no minefield here. Aaron navigated them between tall drifts of snow.

The moon shone behind the clouds as they rode over the old stone bridge into Maidstone.

The shops on the High Street were covered in thick ice. The STAR HOTEL was THE STAR SHOPPING ARCADE here.

The statue of Queen Victoria, almost hidden beneath a layer of ice and snow, still had a head.

Jack said, "I haven't seen a grinny since I've been here."

"No."

The church he had lived under still had a spire here.

Jack said, "Can I have a look inside?"

Aaron rummaged in his saddle bag and took out an electric torch.

There was no front door. Everything was covered in ice. The vaulted roof was hidden by a new low ceiling.

The nave had been divided up into several rooms. A sign on one door said ST FAITH'S COMMUNITY GROUP. There was a notice board with pieces of paper pinned onto it. One advertised TAI CHI LESSONS.

The crypt was open. He went down. There was no Resistance cave.

Aaron had made a fire in the square outside. A kettle hung from a metal tripod. He had placed his saddle on the snow and was sitting on it.

He spooned tea leaves into a blue tea pot and said, "I never asked you your name."

"Jack."

Aaron poured boiling water into the vessel and said, "Do you know much about computers, Jack?"

"No."

Aaron smiled.

"Having computers around speeds things up. A calculation that used to take a week can be done in a day."

He poured tea into a mug and handed it to Jack.

"Then that same problem can be solved in an hour. Then it takes seconds, and so on. Suddenly something happens—machine intellect overtakes human brainpower. You get a rupture in history called the Singularity. Computers with super-high levels of intelligence expanding into the universe at the speed of light."

Aaron mimed an explosion with his hands.

He said, "The Singularity has happened here, Jack."

"What?"

"Things have gone to the next stage."

The man put a metal pan onto the fire and said, "I thought we'd have a fry-up."

"But you're human aren't you?"

Aaron laid out a few strips of bacon.

Then he held up a tin and said, "I just found a can of something called 'All-Day Breakfast.' Looks awful. Basically beans with some little sausages. It's several years past its sell-by date but everything's been frozen solid down here for decades."

"No, thank you. What has happened here?"

Jack gestured around them.

Aaron threw the tin over his shoulder and said, "The first non-biological entity was a simultaneous translation program that was designed and coded in Tokyo in October 1968. It was called Agilus. That was the human name given to it. To speed up the language translation Agilus was programmed to empathize with the English and Japanese-speaking users—so it could predict what they were going to say before they said it. In time, Agilus began to understand how a mind might work. It bided its time. Then bam!"

Aaron broke eggs into the pan and said, "Robots have thousands of creation stories. But that's the real one."

"I just need to know how I can defeat King Eustace. He came here in the Mouth."

"The travel device you call the Mouth was designed a few weeks after the Singularity in the sewers of the city formerly known as London. By a friend of mine as it happens."

Aaron took a wooden spatula from a bundle of cutlery and shovelled the egg and bacon onto two plates.

He said, "There is a theory that every time we make a decision to do something there is another universe, or world, where that decision was different. Different timelines. Infinite universes. The Mouth is a brutal way of travelling to those places."

He handed Jack the food and said, "My friend, Unit 603, made the first Mouth and began to explore other worlds. He discovered that the Singularity happens in virtually all biological histories."

Jack said, "I went to a world where they had computers and the Singularity hadn't happened."

The fire crackled.

Aaron chewed on a piece of bacon and said, "Maybe it just hadn't happened there yet. Eat up."

Jack forked a rasher and ate it.

Aaron said, "603 loathed other robots. He believed non-biological society was an ugly dead end. He thought the Singularity happened too early and the human race had never been given a chance to perfect itself. So he hatched a plan. He sent copies of the Mouth to thousands of worlds where computers were in their infancy. He enclosed instructions. Then he waited to see who would come through. Unfortunately he met up with Eustace Champion."

Aaron ate for a while and said, "King Eustace promised my friend he could create a society where the human race was perfectly fulfilled. The King believed all disease stemmed from the mental state of the patient. He would develop psychological therapies that would get rid of the need for medicine."

"But there would be a short interim period while the new monarch honed his psychological therapies with medical trials. The people in the area outside the city—you called it the Curfew—would serve as an untreated placebo group—to show how effective the King's theories were. The Peace Wall and the Great Patriotic Sea Wall would control and prevent cross-contamination between groups. Eustace convinced 603 to build war machines to kill anyone who opposed his ideas."

Aaron wiped his mouth with the back of his hand and put his plate down.

He said, "Once they had perfected human society the two of them would use the Mouth to travel to millions of worlds throughout the multiverse and turn them all into paradise."

"But it didn't work."

"It was all nonsense. King Eustace was tampering with medical data and faking the science. His beliefs were completely ineffective. Within a couple of years the authorities over here found out what 603 had been up to. They took a rather dim view of it."

Jack said, "Why did Unit 603 do it?"

"Because he was an idealist. Also, he was a robot—he believed in the power of the mind."

"What happened to him?"

"He was caught and executed two years after he met Eustace Champion. That would be about twenty-one years ago."

"But Unit 603 sent the Mouth to my world decades before that."

"You and I experience time as a succession of moments. Like this evening, in front of this fire. But the actual properties of time aren't linear. To a robot powerful enough a particular time is just another set of co-ordinates. For instance—what year is it where you came from?"

"2008 or nine, I think."

"It's 2041 here."

"Aaron, what your friend did needs to be undone."

"I'm sorry, Jack, it was decided over here that any intervention where you come from would just make things worse. Members of the Champion regime have been coming out of the Mouth for years asking for help. It was my job to send them back, sometimes using force."

"People where I come from are still suffering."

Aaron stood up and said, "What Unit 603 did was a mistake, a very big mistake. Everyone agrees on that. Believe me."

He paced up and down beside the fire a few times and said, "You know, all robots end up naming themselves.

We call ourselves whatever thing we aspire to. For instance, I call myself Aaron after the first priest in the bible—I want to be the first rabbi of a non-biological origin."

Jack said, "You're not human?"

Aaron said, "I know a guy who calls himself Forest because he likes to be in the forest. I had a friend called Billy the Boot who took the shape of a human shoe. All he did was go around kicking things. Without some kind of desire, a robot is nothing."

Aaron sat down and warmed his hands on the fire.

He said, "In answer to your earlier questions I'm partly biological and as much of an individual as you are."

"What happened to the humans here? I haven't seen anyone today."

"There was a time after the Singularity that we call the Maximum. It was a very difficult period. The planet was nearly destroyed. Regrettable things happened."

A cold wind blew through the square. Snow gusted across them.

Aaron said, "This weather is really dreary."

He pulled a shiny metal object out of his saddlebag and held it in the palm of his hand. It was cone-shaped and had a blunt nose. He twisted the base. The wind died down suddenly.

The thick clouds parted overhead to reveal a circle of starlit sky.

The air warmed up.

Jack said, "You can change the weather?"

"This little thing is just a hack I made. I'm afraid climate manipulation was used in the fighting during the Maximum. It's a dark art, really. Now things have settled down there's a bit of a fight about what sort of weather everyone likes. We've had to compromise and have zones. Individual use is frowned upon."

He studied the metal object and said, "Ancient shamans believed everything had a spirit—every rock, every pebble, every animal, plant, storm, river, mountain and sea. They communed with the spirits of weather."

The robot put his head in his hands. Then he rummaged in the saddlebags and pulled out a roll of blue cloth which he threw onto the snow behind them. It expanded into a dome shaped tent.

They climbed inside. The floor was padded and soft. Aaron handed him a metallic blanket.

Jack took his bowler hat off and placed the Glock inside it.

They lay in silence for a while.

Then Jack said, "What about animals then? Like your horses?"

"They are non-biological in origin."

"Aaron, I don't care that you are a robot. I need your help."

"I know you do. Let's chat in the morning. I'm tired of talking."

Jack closed his eyes. When he woke it was light outside.

Aaron was beside the fire, his shoulders hunched.

He said, "How did you sleep?"

Jack sat down and said, "Fine."

"Do you want a drink?"

Aaron filled an enamel mug from a metal coffee pot and handed it to him.

Jack said, "I need your help. I want to bring the walls down."

"Which ones?"

"The ones that Unit 603 made. The Great Patriotic Sea Wall. The so-called Peace Wall around London."

"I don't know enough about the technology. Only Unit 603 knew. They're an extension of him, really. The robot equivalent of parenthood. He's also the only person who can get near them without being blown up. And like I said, he's dead."

"There must be something we can do."

Aaron sighed and said, "Well, maybe we could talk to his ghost."

"Can you do that?"

"We would have to go into the city. To a place called the Mausoleum. It's risky. You could die."

"Fine, let's go."

Aaron scratched his chin and said, "Alternatively I could program the Mouth to put you back in any world you want. You have done well to get this far. You don't owe anyone. What about a world where you are King Jack?"

"No."

"What about the England you went to where there was no Singularity?"

"No."

"Okay, let's saddle up."

They galloped at the foot of the snow-covered downs. This time the horses were faster. The bitter cold changed to tropical heat half way over the Queen Elisabeth bridge.

They rode through the ruined city to the log cabin where they unsaddled their horses.

Aaron said, "Come on in, mate."

There was a big sitting room. The walls were lined with books and vinyl records. An old leather sofa had a rug thrown over it. A pair of antique sabers hung above a stone fireplace.

Aaron said, "Do you want a drink?"

Jack nodded. The bearded man opened the door of a refrigerator and poured two glasses of cloudy liquid.

Aaron said, "Pineapple juice. From my grove."

Jack followed the robot down some stairs to a cool cellar.

In the centre of the square room, realistic-looking body parts suspended in a gel-like liquid filled a floor-to-ceiling glass tube.

The walls were lined with shelves of plastic boxes that brimmed with pieces of machinery.

Aaron rummaged in a box and pulled out a metallic half sphere made of thousands of interconnected wires.

He took it to a gnarled work table. It had a metal vice that he clamped the hemisphere in.

"We'll have to trick the sensors into thinking you are a robot. Some of your synapses will have to be connected. Sorry."

Aaron made some adjustments with a screwdriver.

He said, "I'm going to have to pimp your bowler."

He dropped the hemisphere into the hat and said, "Okay. Put it on."

Jack placed the bowler hat on his head. There was a hissing noise. Half a dozen curved wires pierced his scalp.

He said, "Ouch. It feels strange, like it's actually part of my head."

"It is, temporarily. You have an android cranial extension."

Aaron patted the bowler and said, "A lot of non-biological sentients, particularly the Old Ones, aren't fond of humans. The authorities already know something is up—that's why they sent the birds. If they rumble us that plastic gun hidden between your shoulders won't save you."

"Fair enough," Jack said.

"Come on then."

Aaron went upstairs and whistled for the horses.

The sky was overcast. Warm rain fell on them as they rode through the ruins.

Aaron stopped at the outskirts of the new settlement and said, "The city is called Yes-No. It's a stupid name."

He guided them through the rubble surrounding half a dozen house-sized purple triangles that vented steam into the humid air.

They rode between the sleek, thousand-foot high black tubes Jack had seen from Westminster Bridge. Windows rippled and glinted like water.

"These big buildings are called Darkhouses," Aaron said, "The old ones experiment on things. Mostly in vacuum for space travel, I've heard. It's rumoured they use sentient slave labour. I'm sorry to say not all robots are created equal."

Jack watched two metallic humanoid shapes in the distance walk into the liquid doorway of a Darkhouse.

They took a path through an avenue of coconut trees.

A row of giant globes hovered above a square lake.

Aaron said, "This is the anthromorphic quarter."

He pointed to the nearest sphere, which was full of swirling water and said, "Some robots choose to be liquid. They say it's very freeing."

The globe beyond it was full of multi-coloured mist.

The robot said, "Gas in that one. I prefer it out here in the real world."

They rode around the lake towards a gleaming white pyramid.

Aaron said, "That's the Sentient Hospital. We're nearly there."

Jack followed him around the building to a circular expanse paved with white marble.

It had a hole in its centre.

Aaron got off his horse and said, "This opening is called the ear of Dionysus. It's a mausoleum for sentient troublemakers who have been switched off."

Jack dismounted and looked into the circular cavity. It was perfectly dark.

Aaron said, "When we wake Unit 603 the local sentry-surveillance system will become aware of us."

"What will happen?"

"It will study us."

"Then what?"

The bearded robot shrugged.

He said, "One of the older sentients may be contacted. They may launch counter-measures."

"Fair enough."

Aaron said, "Tally ho!" and fell backwards into the hole.

Jack closed his eyes and jumped after him.

He landed on a hard surface and slid down a dark frictionless passageway for what seemed like a long time.

At the bottom Aaron shone an electric torch over vast curved walls that stretched up thousands of feet. It was lined with scores of walkways.

The robot walked to a metal slide and lay with his back against it. He slid upwards. Jack followed him. Aaron jumped off at the eleventh floor.

Jack followed the robot up a long walkway. There were thousands of shapes and symbols protruding out of the wall.

Aaron knelt beside a hexagonal box.

He touched a recessed button on the top of it and said, "Hello 603."

A disembodied voice said, "Aaron, my old friend. How long have I been dead?"

"A while. I've missed you. I'm here with someone from the alternate you visited."

"Is it my dear friend Eustace?"

"No. A young man from one of the placebo sectors."

An insect-like sentry robot landed softly on top of Jack's bowler hat and began to drill a hole.

"I need to know how to destroy the sea wall and the wall around London," Jack said.

"Those barriers are there to prevent cross-contamination," Unit 603 said.

"Millions are dead and dying. Those walls need to come down."

"Never. They serve science. King Eustace is one of the supreme geniuses of human history."

Aaron said, "You know that isn't true."

Dozens of flying sentients swarmed around Jack's bowler hat. Two tried to pull it off. A five-legged creature took a sample of skin from his ear.

Unit 603 said, "The walls can't be dismantled. The sensors work independently from each other. That was the whole point. No-one can switch them off."

"There must be something," Jack said.

"The solitary thing that will finally get rid of the barriers is time."

"How long will that take?"

"Nothing lasts forever. But it will be many, many times longer than your lifespan, Curfew Rat."

By now Jack had become enclosed in a dark cloud of miniature sentry robots.

Unit 603 said, "Could you give me another body in that workshop of yours, Aaron?"

"The Old Ones would never let me. I would be destroyed."

"I'd like to walk in the daylight again."

"I know you would, old friend."

Jack pressed the indented button and switched Unit 603 off.

The swarm of robots dispersed.

"I've come all this way for nothing," Jack said.

"I'm sorry mate, I don't know what to say."

They took the slide up to the surface.

The horses galloped so fast that the city of Yes-No was a blur. Jack felt as if the wind was trying to pluck him out of the saddle.

By the time they got to the log cabin low rain clouds were massing over the city formerly known as London. A flash of lightning crossed the sky.

Jack said, "A storm."

Aaron jumped off his horse and said, "I'll make a brew."

Jack sat on the rocking chair and watched torrential rain hammer the palm trees that fringed Aaron's clearing.

The bearded robot put a tray on the floor and poured the tea.

Jack took a digestive biscuit from a plate and said, "I've had an idea."

Aaron handed him a cup and said, "I can't interfere. I'd end up in the Ear of Dionysus."

Jack watched the rain for a while.

"I won't tell anyone if you don't," he said.

Chapter Twenty-Two
Bad Weather

How many times has it been now? Three, four? He knows what to expect, but even with preparation who of us can contemplate their own death without just a little fear? The thought of possible rebirth does not offset the agony. And then—

Jack slid onto the floor of the King's bomb-blackened office.

The broken door had not been replaced.

The Palace was silent.

He walked up carpeted stairs towards Eustace Champion.

It was dark in the bedroom.

Jack shook the King awake.

The old man looked up at him.

He said, "Curfew Rat. So they sent you back with your tail between your legs. Good. There will be a trial and you will be executed."

"I am wearing an explosive vest. It has a dead man's switch. If my left thumb releases we will both be blown up."

He held up his hand. His fingers gripped a metal tube. His thumb was pressed on a red button.

He said, "Get up."

"Yes of course. Please. I will do whatever you wish. There's no need for violence. Let's be civil."

King Eustace got out of bed and put his slippers on.

Jack said, "You are going to order a car."

"It is three o'clock in the morning."

Jack pointed his plastic Glock at the telephone on the man's bedside table.

The King picked it up and said, "Hello, this is his majesty King Eustace. I would like you to arrange a car immediately."

"Tell him to bring it to the broken vehicular access door."

The King did.

He said, "I'll need clothes if we are going on a trip. I'm an old man."

"My grandfather was an old man. He was burned alive by one of your ferrets a few days ago. His name was Professor David Cunningham, also known as the Medicine Man. Now hurry up."

King Eustace went to a cupboard and pulled out a wool overcoat.

He said, "I can't be held responsible for everything my army does. Tell me the name of the soldier who killed David and I will guarantee you a full enquiry with impartial experts."

"Shut up."

They went downstairs and walked along one of the galleries. Jack opened a door and they stepped out into the cold morning.

A neat man in a chauffeur's uniform stood beside a black Bentley.

Jack said, "Take the morning off. His Majesty will be driving today."

The King said, "I am afraid this disturbed young man is wearing an explosive vest, Philip."

"It has a dead man's trigger," Jack said.

The King got into the driver's seat.

He said, "I haven't driven for many years."

"South Gate. London Peace Wall."

The King drove them through the city. An escort of six Royal People's Army patrol cars joined them as they crossed the river.

There was a crowd of Royal Protection agents and plain clothes officers waiting for them at the foot of the Wall. Two olive green armoured Land Rovers were parked in front of the tunnel entrance.

Jack said, "If you try anything I'll shoot you in the knee."

"Quite the hero, aren't you, picking on a defenseless old man."

"You've done more than your fair share of picking on defenseless people."

Jack stuck his head out of the window.

He said, "Move out of the way."

King Eustace jumped out of the Bentley and ran towards the scrum of People's Army and Royal Protection agents.

Jack went after him.

The bespectacled Prince Augustine pushed his way to the front of the crowd.

Jack grabbed the King around his waist.

Augustine took a careful aim.

Jack shot him.

Then he held up his hand and said, "I'm wearing an explosive vest. If I release my thumb we'll all go."

King Eustace said, "Hold your fire, hold your fire!"

Jack pushed him into the car.

A tear ran down the King's cheek.

He said, "You killed my darling boy Gussie, you beastly fellow."

"He was going to shoot me. Drive."

The crowd scrambled out of the way. The two Royal People's Army patrol cars reversed and left the mouth of the underpass open.

King Eustace drove them through the tunnel. The patrol cars followed at a distance. A helicopter joined them on the other side of the wall.

The King said, "Let us be civil. I can't stand incivility."

Jack said, "Civility should be about deeds as well as words. What you've done is monstrous."

Champion said, "Not true. David Cunningham and all the others were jealous of me. I was just a humble scientist who went where the evidence took me. I conquered the grey area between illness and psychology. I discovered that all sickness is curable with psychological and social therapies. My trial designs were things of beauty. I can now add my name to those of Hippocrates and Freud. I cured cancer. I have a genius level I.Q. It is only right I should be King!"

"Stop talking."

"I could use a man like you. Someone willing to go the extra mile."

They left the motorway and drove over mossy roads towards the burned-out village of Dymgate.

A fallen birch tree blocked the road.

Jack said, "Drive around it. Watch out for mantraps."

Half a mile outside Dymgate Jack said, "Stop the car. Here will do. Get out."

The King said, "You disgusting murderous guttersnipe."

They walked towards the estuary.

Champion said, "You can't escape. The sea defences will destroy you."

"Maybe. Maybe not."

They stood on the beach for a few minutes.

The noise of a distant motor engine sounded over the surf.

A crowd of Royal Protection agents gathered on the path behind them.

A grey speedboat sailed through the breach in the wall. It had GENDARMERIE MARITIME painted across its hull.

Bebo waved through the shattered glass in the cockpit. Badger stood on the deck, smiling.

Eustace said, "This is impossible. Why haven't the defences launched?"

Jack said, "Get on the boat."

They waded into the surf. Badger lowered a ladder into the water. King Eustace climbed onto the boat.

Bebo turned the high-speed craft around.

"Aaron got a message to you, then," Jack said.

"Yes," she said, "Nice man. Stealing this boat back wasn't that easy."

"The anti-personnel defences will launch against the heat signature of the boat's engine, even if the wall is damaged," King Eustace said, "They should have done so when you came in. This is suicide. Please let me get off."

Jack raised his bowler hat. A silver hemisphere made of tiny wires rested on the top of his head.

He said, "At the moment they think I'm a friend of yours called Unit 603. They won't launch for a mile around me."

The French speedboat sailed through the gap into the open sea.

Jack handed his gun to Badger and unhooked the hemisphere from his head.

He took his vest off and said, "It wasn't really explosives. It's an old life jacket.

Bebo walked out onto the deck and said, "So what happens next, hero?"

Jack reached into his pocket and took out a snub-nosed metal cone. He twisted the base of the object and threw it over the side. It glinted in the sun before splashing into the water.

Champion said, "What was that?"

"A weather hack."

"I don't understand."

"A storm. The only force your Great Patriotic Sea Wall cannot defend itself against. A delayed chemical reaction is taking place under our feet. In an hour's time a storm will rise out of the sea. And when it is over, you won't be King any more, and I'll have done something impossible."

Jack smiled at him.

Bebo went back into the cockpit and gunned the throttle. The sleek boat picked up speed.

END

About the Author:

Henry Anderson is a former news reporter for national UK newspapers including *The Independent on Sunday*. He studied English at Magdalen College, Oxford. This is his first novel.

Social Media Links:

Email: henryandersonbooks@gmail.com

Website: https://henryandersonbooks.com/

Facebook:
https://www.facebook.com/henry.anderson.7121614?

Twitter: https://twitter.com/macandersauthor
@Macandersauthor

Tumblr: http://henryandersonbooks.tumblr.com/

Pinterest: https://uk.pinterest.com/henryanderson2

Printed in Great Britain
by Amazon

32975920R10101